the Men
Went to Town

The Day the Men Went to Town

is the

**CJCB Radio
Book of the Year**

Sponsored by CJCB Radio, the CJCB Radio
Book of the Year has been established to promote
good writing and publishing in Cape Breton.
Previous recipients are:

Ellison Robertson
The Last Gael and Other Stories

Anselme Chiasson
Rosie Aucoin Grace, translator
*The Seven-Headed Beast
and Other Acadian Tales
from Cape Breton Island*

Sheldon Currie
The Glace Bay Miners' Museum—The Novel

The Day the Men Went to Town

Went to Town

16 STORIES
BY WOMEN FROM CAPE BRETON

SELECTED BY RONALD CAPLAN

Breton Books
Wreck Cove, Cape Breton Island

Editor: Ronald Caplan
Design: Ronald Caplan & Bonnie Thompson
Cover Photograph: "La Fume" by Carol Kennedy

The following stories are reprinted with the permission of the authors and/or publishers:
"Sunburn" is from *Holy Days of Obligation*, published by Nuage Editions, 1998. "Cave Paintings" is from *Fall on Your Knees*, published by Alfred A. Knopf Canada, 1996. "Passage by Water" appeared in *From a High Thin Wire*, published by NeWest Publishers Ltd., 1982. "Home Fires" is from *After the Angel Mill*, published by Cormorant Books, 1995. It also appeared in *Room of One's Own*, Vancouver, 1995. "Batter My Heart" first appeared in *The Fiddlehead*, Autumn 1994, and will be included in *Play the Monster Blind*, Doubleday Canada, 2000. "Harvest" appeared in a slightly different form in *Woman in the Rock*, published by Gynergy Books, 1993. "Every Girl Turns into Her Mother" first appeared in *The Antigonish Review*, Summer-Autumn 1995. "The Day the Men Went to Town" is from *Stories from the Woman from Away*, published by Breton Books, 1996. "Overburden" first appeared in *The Antigonish Review*, Summer 1997.

LE CONSEIL DES ARTS
DU CANADA
DEPUIS 1957

THE CANADA COUNCIL
FOR THE ARTS
SINCE 1957

**We acknowledge the support of
the Canada Council for the Arts for our publishing program.
We also acknowledge support from Cultural Affairs,
Nova Scotia Department of Tourism and Culture.**

Canadian Cataloguing in Publication Data

The day the men went to town

ISBN 1-895415-43-8

1. Short stories, Canadian (English) — Women authors.* 2. Short stories, Canadian (English) — Nova Scotia — Cape Breton Island.* 3. Canadian fiction (English) — 20th century.* I. Caplan, Ronald, 1942-

PS8329.5.N6D3 1999   C813'.01089287   C99-950194-1
PR9197.33.W65D38 1999

Contents

Publisher's Note

I HAD JUST PUBLISHED the complete works of Tessie Gillis. She was the woman who tore back the curtain on Cape Breton Island, writing a deeper and darker portait of life there than anyone had taken on before.

After her books were out, I started thinking about the recent fame of several other Cape Breton writers such as Lynn Coady, Jean McNeil and Ann-Marie MacDonald—and I wondered what a book comprised of writing from them and lesser-known Cape Breton women would look like. That gave me the frame for the search for this book.

The rule I set for myself was simple: I wanted strong writing by women who have a significant attachment to Cape Breton, no matter where they now live in the world. They didn't have to be born in Cape Breton, and many included here weren't. And they did not have to write about Cape Breton—and, for this collection at least, a lot of them don't.

The stories in *The Day the Men Went to Town* are about fisherwomen and aliens from space, the poignancy of family life and tragedy in the coal mines. They are about several approaches to love. Many of these writers have already earned serious attention in Canadian literature, some have achieved a bit of fame—and several will be discoveries.

The title comes from a story by Tessie Gillis, honouring the woman who started it all.

Ronald Caplan
Cape Breton's Magazine
Wreck Cove

*H*arvest

CLAUDIA GAHLINGER

Scullerymaids

*T*HE MORNING was a beautiful bottomless bowl but empty. So empty it could make you forget you'd ever felt that sudden blooming, that sense of being on the verge—when you'd caught something miraculous—of knowing the ocean whole. This feeling, if it made a sound, would go *wommm*, as in woman, and womb. Like marsupials we could carry the sea in our bellies.

This morning might in truth have been full, teeming with timid, suspicious or aloof codfish and untold millions of mysteries. But I doubted it. For months now Ariel and I had been catching codfish, making a living at it. But it was easy to forget this. Slouched on the gunnel, yanking at the line, I examined my boots all morning for possible defects. Found none of those either.

Into the emptiness crept fishermen's opinions. Two women together are two women alone. And women alone who venture out to sea in a twenty-foot open boat are a sly mocking at Potency. Women will wander cheerfully into squalls. Sit patient over schools of mud and sea urchins. Catch nothing but dogfish and then feel sorry for them.

We just don't belong on the water. Some say alone, some say at all. Our flesh is too soft, our will too weak, our body cycles are embarrassing. Then there's our need of a bucket and privacy to pee in instead of pissing manly over the side—

It may be true about the peeing, but the rest is a private matter between ourselves and the sea, isn't it?

Ariel held herself proud all this while. She gazed at the mountain-lines unperturbed, a professor interpreting emptiness her own way. "People think fish are our evolutionary inferiors," she said. "But when you're sitting in a boat like a lonely corner at a party you recognize them for what they are: guileless. Enviably simple. Such unity of purpose. It's ironic," she added, "to love the fish yet want to kill them."

I didn't want to kill them, of course. Just catch them. And sell them.

I was praying to the line again, Oh make this beautiful bowl full, when Ariel jerked forward, pouncing on something invisible. Then she relaxed and began to draw light and quick. "Oh," she said, disappointed before even a first glimpse.

"What is it?"

"Nothing," she said, still drawing. "Something that wriggles. Flutters. Too light for a codfish."

Sea cucumber. Sea urchin. Sea butterfly: that would be a change.

"Probably a pollock," Ariel said.

Oh the little pollock. Mediocrity of the sea. Grey, soft and frivolous, forever ready to hop aboard unasked. Since they're not worth a cent at the size we catch them we work pollock off our hooks and send them home. Mediocrity, damaged in transit. Must we mark this day with a small act of sadism?

But breaking free of water the silver rising on Ariel's line proved to be something entirely different. A shimmying, rich-coloured jewel flew off her hook and hit the deck.

"Well..." came Ariel's stuttered laugh.

Wommm. It was a Persian fish. An Arabian Nights fish. A smooth bar of cobalt blue with emerald stripes, faint opal rainbows on its silvery underside. For a second it held still, as if shocked or amazed, then began to swim hard, drumming sidelong across the deck.

Curtains of myth and fairy tale fell sheer before my eyes. I thought, This must be the kind of fish that carries a ring in its belly. A golden ring, inscribed with a plea for help: there's a queen, and she's labouring under a curse that keeps her a scullerymaid. And rescuing the queen would in turn release us from catching fish. This happy, humble task with its hideous aspect: diverting creatures each from its own urgent message about life.

We dropped our lines again but no reply. Still. "They've started to come into the bay," said Ariel happily. "Too bad we don't have our mackerel jigs. We might as well head in." She pulled at the outboard cord and pointed the *Anicca*'s bow at the channel mouth, three or so kilometres distant. "Here, you steer," she said. Then, "Mackerel. Great. I'll fillet it for lunch."

Which she did, tossing the guts to the gulls.

No sign of a ring. If there was a queen she would go on as a scullerymaid. And we would go on fishing.

Mackerelle

THEY BEGAN TO SWARM into the bay under cover of water. Sometimes when they rose up we'd see their schooling agitation from shore: dark patches of them, frittering near the surface. Close up from aboard the *Anicca* they appeared as a broad, sinister slashing like an arena of miniature sharks fighting.

We would venture out in the early dark. Motor over a calm sea. Pull on dayglo orange mackerel gloves made for men with immense fingers, the insides cool and clammy from the day before. Unwind lines strung with five hooks and a lead weight into the water. As it slithers down, drifts down, meanders, dawdles like a leaf from a tree, you give the line random yanks. Because, while codfish gravitate to the bottom, mackerel shift up and down as if they were adrift themselves.

"Nothing here," Ariel would say. "We'll try further out."

Try again. This time the slithering line buckles to nothing, the lead weight has been stolen clean away—no, a sharp tug reveals that the knaves are caught.

"Here they are," Ariel whispers.

This is surely a hair-raising business.

A blind quivering sense of them, like intuition or dream memory or words on the tip of the tongue, rises reluctant—surrendering—rebellious. Some stealthy hand-over-hand hauling and they appear at last: one or two shards of silver, spiralling. Draw against them, with them, against them until they break clear of their element. Hoist them in and flip them off the hooks. They bang against the deck—hold still for a second—then begin drumming, vigorous and uncanny.

Drop the line again quick. Hoist and drop, haul and shake, the fish spin across the deck five and one and three at a time. When we've let down our hooks again and again catching fish every time, "Here we are," Ariel will say, meaning we're not just transient over a random scatter of mackerel now but afloat over a school of them. I imagine them rippling in the current like a field of silvery oats in a breeze.

So we fish. And so we drift. And so we forget who or where we are. Until sometimes, looking up, we find ourselves among other boats like a parking lot of wobbling cars, all occupied by fishers bringing in mackerel. Families, all ages and sizes. Married couples jigging side by each. Great splinter-sided hulls holding crews of three or four men, all surly and shy. I steal glimpses of their labouring and try to learn.

Old-time fishers move without doubt. They haul the mackerel out of the water easy as lifting a clothesline strung with flimsy slippers. Holding the line in a two-handed arch they give it a sharp jerk that sends a rain of slippers to the deck, then scurry the line into the water again, all without having caught those flying needle-fine hooks in their shirt cuffs or on the gunnel ridge or in the bare skin of their wrists, let alone snarling them in among themselves like a catfight the way I will mine.

Ariel stands beside me, a benign and single-minded huntress. Her back straight, her muscles sure, she lifts and sheds fish from her line in earnest.

Me, I like to see the fish as music. Lift the line high, feel their pull and know their weight—their vigorous, portentous music—in every muscle. Bring the line down like a conductor signalling the entire orchestra to pounce on a chord and every note comes down brilliantly. Sometimes this works.

All together our boats bob amiably. It's a country dance: we hang out in the fishlot, dancing a syncopated jig. Doing The Mackerelle. Haul and thresh, haul and thresh—it is a dying art, small-time fishing being a failing economy. The seiners can scoop up fish in two-ton mouthfuls. But this looks and feels graceful as any act of harvest or animal of prey. Why do all the small fine movements have to end?

Nothing

FRENZIED ONSLAUGHTS OF THEM end all too soon. Boats disperse to new spots. We drift over flutters—brief showers—mere spits of fish, sharp and flighty as déjà vu. Then nothing, again. The abrupt and dreaded nothing.

To lose a codfish as it spirals up on your line is despair and abandonment. But a drift of mackerel interrupted brings giddy frustration. Breathlessness. The blues.

"We've wandered out of their pasture," I say. "We've drifted apart. Grown estranged. The sea is sad cowboy country. The fish are a hurtin' song."

A skipper's job is to counter their crew's addlebrained remarks with common sense. Ariel scans the water. "It's our featherbaits," she decides. She means these new ones with the long red and yellow plumes. "The fish are down in the saloon, saying, Think we're cheap? And laughing. That chilling mackerel laugh." She shudders. "That bloodcurdling. Mackerel. Cackle."

You'd never guess Ariel was old enough to be my mother. Well, nearly.

Bells ring in my armpits, in my hands. We could fill this emptiness easy: yell at the mountains like seagulls, like one-year-olds. If there were trees around we could forget the fish—or forget the trees, we could swing from each other's limbs, hollering and cheeping like monkeys.

The Line

A DRIZZLY CALM MORNING. *Anicca* carried us out the channel onto the sea. Tired, we moved between two greys: heavy dark of ocean asleep, damp light of air awakening, both of them soft to the eyes and skin as a herring gull's feathers.

Far ahead of us the pretty two-tiered seiners floated like fogged wedding cakes toward the horizon. Closer ahead the small boats—humbler predators—forayed toward the Point or the lighthouse, the two destinations a dozen kilometres apart.

Ariel might decide to join them. But first and as usual she would check near the green buoy, just half a mile from the channel mouth. "If the fish are biting," she liked to say, "why not get them close to home?"

So close here we could see the house up on the hill and wonder which of us forgot to turn off the kitchen light.

Anicca still in a curve of her settling, we let down our hooks.

Unwind the line reluctantly. Down into dreams below, under the hull, in fearful darkness. How can we know what lurks down there, waiting to foist itself on us, emerging monstrous out of our own imaginations?

Ominous nothing turned to conundrum quick. The lines went slack as though the leads had been bitten off. Tug at them and a weight grabs heavy, the line swoons—*wommm*—heavy as the drag of gravity when the earth seems to draw the blood down from your womb, nearly drawing you to your knees, only now there's no ache only ponderousness, your senses all plunge underwater.

"Here they are," Ariel gasped.

Strain at them. They give in—resist—give in and break into air at last, mackerel after all, and "Hoo! They're big."

Shun them from the hooks onto the deck. No hesitation but they begin thundering, awesome and unnerving as black and grey bars of iron knocking on your bedroom floor in the night.

We dropped our hooks again. They were taken so fast the lines swooped in great arcs through the water.

"Here we are."

Time to harvest. Bring in the sheaves. Thresh the fish from the lines, saying "Hoo," and "Huh," and "Aah..." with relief as every knot in the mind is undone.

In happy labouring there is no haste or delay.... The morning passed out of time....

The deck was blue and silver, drumming and fibrillating and rumbling with slapping fish when Ariel looked up. "Whoa," she called out. That stuttering laugh.

The current had nearly hauled us up against the green half-mile buoy. Close enough for introductions. But Ariel just repeated, "Whoa." As if the buoy were going anywhere. Portly it sat. Colossal, blinking, ironic. Ariel started the outboard; we went bowing backward out of its presence.

We filled the hiatus with long-neglected chores. Blow the nose and doff the cap. Shed and bundle the oilskin jacket. Take a quick look around at the day.

The mist had lifted, the sky was a soft high haze. The hills had turned green. The lights of the village had blended with daylight. Breakfast time. Prayer time. The houses and St. Mary's Church were a dream of habit and faith. Land was the place where you could imagine God protecting you.

The sea was placid enough, though. And apparently empty. Boats from the Point were motoring toward the lighthouse. Boats at the lighthouse had decided to try for the Point.

Complacent now as a brood hen the *Anicca* turned and settled again.

We dropped our lines; they collapsed and tensed. Whatever fish are wont to do when wise to one's tricks or indisposed or just not hungry any more, these fish had not done. No.

"Queens for a Day," Ariel gasped, hauling her line with dayglo pinkies extended.

"Patient as a Mackerel, they say."

"Forgiving as a Mackerel. Patient as a Pollock."

Their silver turned visible now just two or three fathoms down. The whole field had risen.

Boat and all, the morning turned into a recurring dream. Our restless tossing and threshing brought ever more shimmying protest, more jubilant slaughter. Jolt the line, the fish fly, fish come apart at the gills. The joy of harvest side by side with the horror of killing makes for an impossible dance that sheds the mind again and again. No place for thought, just the pride of the hunter in the rhythm of her body.

The mackerel kept crowding our lines and they were still hefty ones. They were beginning to be an illustration of that saying, Be careful what you wish for you might get it.

Not shunned any more at the party but backed into a corner by nonstop talkers we began to sigh and roll our eyes. Our patience turned saint-like. The fish were tireless petitioners. They crept up our boots, rumbled three deep on the deck, spattered blood water.

The nylon line was wearing out my thumb and jigging finger. It creased the glove into the groove worn into my hand by the line creasing the glove, and more fish were waiting below.

It's like the tyranny of a narrative line, I thought. Moving forward, forward, forward can seem just like standing still. Then why do people prefer stories with plots over ones that drift, spiralling over fish or no fish?

The sun stood near noon. The water's rocking and the day's warmth gentled us toward sleep. Ariel and I each slogged through the fish once to lie down on the bow. We jigged languidly for a while, staring at the sky. There's a game adults should play more often: you rest your head on each other's bellies; when one of you starts to laugh the others are done for. Lying back on the bow, Ariel and I rumbled the same way.

A song would help us counter this lullaby. A hearty chant, like the chant of women washing clothes in a river, or pounding roots for flour. Or swishing and thumping new-woven cloth in a milling frolic. But we couldn't manage a syllable.

Dream a wish-fulfillment dream about not mackerel fishing. Hot, weary-boned, sore-muscled, it was time to wake up. The mackerel were up to our calves now, trapping us. We were fishing on the spot, and who'd caught whom?

The *Anicca* no longer rocked. She wobbled and heaved.

"Maybe we've done it," I said. I meant, maybe we'd caught more than our share. Maybe, according to some universal law, we had gone over the limit. This mass of fish was about to shift, rolling us over. Hell is a place where harvests go to waste.

"Maybe," Ariel agreed, following her own train of thought. Hoisting another full line luxurious as an Amazon she sighed and said, "Is there no rest."

Close on the heels of her lament a gap opened. For a moment our hooks hung idle. Ariel hauled hers out lickety-split. "Wind it up," she said. "Let's go."

Wind It Up

THE DAY HAD BLOSSOMED. An oblique sun shone through the haze. Warm breezes billowed over blue water. Hefty *Anicca's* prow cut proudly into the sea heading home.

I could let go the narrative line right now. Here at the happy prospect of home. But what is a caught fish without a boast? And what about the waiting wharf hands?

"Wait'll they get a load of us," I said.

"We should frown," said Ariel. "Look bored, tough, disgusted. We wouldn't want them to think we're gloating."

"Right."

Anicca wallowed into the channel, a cornucopia bearing our harvest, our silverblue and bloodred charnel. Then she heaved into the wharf's shadow, and something odd happened: as if at the flick of a shutter, the jewel fish turned black and white as commodities.

We were the first boat in. Jack, Cyril and Jimmy emerged from the Co-op office and the ice room. They gathered overhead. Their eyes widened; their mouths opened; their hands reached out to grab our lines. "Jesus," muttered Jack. "Better get the shovels," said Jimmy.

Ariel and I busied ourselves with this and that, scowling murderously the whole time. Until—look here.

Old Mary Alice MacNeil, on her after-dinner stroll, had come floating up behind the guys. Her eyes were black and warm and bright. Her teeth grinned like monuments. Her husky voice gusted over to us, not wearing a shred of decency.

"That's right," she shouted. "You show these guys you can do it!"

So we broke open our happiness. We shovelled our mucky fish into boxes and got them hoisted onto the scales.

"A jesus ton," Cyril reported, at which Jimmy offered smokes.

We all sat around puffing for a while, not saying anything, just nodding the occasional decisive nod and grinning. Then Ariel started the outboard and turned *Anicca* around.

Light as plumed fancy featherbaits we glided back onto the sea. Washed the bloodslush out the scupper. Scrubbed the mire of scales from our oilskins and doused each other clean, sending a gasp of cool down the neck in mischief and in gratitude.

Oh but lucky Queen. Oh but lucky us—

*S*unburn

SUSAN ZETTELL

*C*LIFF GIBSON PULLS HIS CAR into the driveway that separates his lawn from Frank's. Frank is in the back seat with Vern Snyder. Vern's brother Gus is in the front seat with Cliff. Gus needed to be in the front because he was feeling fragile, having drunk too much rye over the weekend. There is a line of dried vomit that starts at Gus' window, runs across Frank's and straight down to the back of the car; Gus stuck his head out to get sick as they drove along the highway. Frank is a bit embarrassed about this, hates the smell too, but doesn't let on. His feet hurt enough to distract him from the smell and the mess.

The motor coughs twice, then stops. As he opens his door, Frank winces. He turns, lifts both feet over the edge of the door frame and gingerly places them, side by side, flat down onto the asphalt. He can feel the heat from the pavement right through his shoes. He leans forward at the waist, grabs onto the frame and hoists himself up. Frank never swears, rarely blasphemes, but he is close to it today.

Already the children are around him and he hopes they will not accidentally trample his feet. Not even bump them gently.

"How many fish did you catch? Are there any big ones? Daddy, did you catch any? What's that smell?"

The sound of their voices mingles with the thud of the car doors as they are closed, Gus' groan as he settles into a lawn chair on

11

Cliff's front porch, the tick of the car's cooling engine, the whine and slap of screen doors as the women come out of the houses and gather around the edges of the crowd. Frank looks down, concentrates so hard on his sore feet, that he hears these sounds distinctly as though they are happening inside his head instead of outside it. He looks up and sees Elizabeth, his wife, standing beside Cliff's wife, Helen. Veronica, Frank's youngest child, is wedged on Elizabeth's hip. Elizabeth smiles at him, concern showing in the lift of an eyebrow.

"I sunburned my feet."

He says this above the noises of the children. He says this to Elizabeth only. He moves to step toward her and winces again. She winces too, looks down at his feet, looks up and mouths, "How?" But there is the hint of a smile at the edges of her lips. She shakes her head and looks down again. Frank knows she is laughing.

Elizabeth's smile disappears. Frank sees her look around, spin her body in an agitated sweep, Veronica almost tipping out of her arms. She is looking at all of the children gathered around the car.

"Frank, do you see David? David! DAVID! Kids, help me find David."

Frank groans as he watches the children begin the search in a delighted, chaotic way.

David is their three-year-old hellion. He learned to walk early, climbed everything, including the doorways, which he scaled by placing a foot on each side of the frame and inching one foot then the other upwards. David dropped Plasticine down the heating vents and tried to stick bobby pins into the electrical sockets. He broke his leg when he was one—fell out of the high chair. Slipped out of the harness, slouched downward then slid onto the floor, his arms pointed up in the air. He screamed when he landed. He didn't stop screaming until they'd put him out at the hospital to set his leg. Not one of the other first four kids, nor the one after, had got out of that harness!

Even the cast didn't slow David down. He loved to make noise, so he crawled as fast as he could, skirting carpets and sticking to the bare hardwood floors. A bump was followed by a loud thump. Bump-THUMP, bump-THUMP, bump-THUMP. He'd stop, sit on his bum, look around at his audience. The other children adored David, and when he laughed and clapped his hands at his own performance, they laughed and clapped too.

"I bet there're still dents in my hardwood floors from that cast."

"What's that, Frank?"

Vern has a handful of fishing poles. He extracts Frank's and hands it to him. Frank reaches out, takes it in his hand. The handle swings over and hits his foot. His lips pull into a firm thin line.

"It's David. Elizabeth can't find him. Guess I'd better give her a hand. I'll get my stuff in a few minutes, Vern."

"I'll help look, too."

Vern—the whole neighbourhood, for that matter—knows about David. Vern takes Frank's pole and leans it with the rest against the car.

"Cliff, come help Frank find David. He got away from Elizabeth again."

Elizabeth sticks her head out of the doorway.

"Frank, get in here. David's locked himself in the bathroom. I can't get him to open the door."

Elizabeth disappears. Vern and Cliff cut straight over the lawn and into Frank's house. The screen door slaps wildly behind them. WHAP-WHAP-WHAP! Frank's lips get thinner.

"I'll have to fix that," he says out loud to no one.

Frank hobbles as quickly as he can on his swollen feet. He stops, sits on the grass and very slowly takes off a running shoe. He can't stand the way it rubs the blisters on his skin.

"Feels like sandpaper," he mutters.

Even the long blades of grass that brush the sides of his now bare foot feel like razors slicing at the too tender skin.

"Fishing. Fishing. Think about the fishing, Frank." He says this to himself, under his breath.

Frank struggles with a knot in the lace of the other shoe and remembers how clear the weather was on Sunday morning. Clear and warm. A steady light breeze kept the worst of the bugs away without disturbing the fish or making the casting difficult. They had breakfast at the camp, plus a splash of rye in their coffee. No reason not to. Just to get them going. Vern splashed rye onto his hands, too, then onto his face like aftershave.

"It'll either kill the damn bugs or they'll go away happy," he said.

Gus must have had a few extra shots at breakfast that Frank didn't notice, because he was asleep under a tree fifteen minutes after his first cast hit the water. In fact Gus stayed hammered or sleeping it off for the whole trip, then vomited all the way home in the car. Frank didn't have a whole lot of sympathy for him, that's for sure.

Cliff and Vern crossed the river and walked a half-mile up to the old willow pool. Frank decided to fish along the shore. With Gus asleep, the only sounds came from the water as it ran over the rocks, the breeze as it whispered through the eel grass, and the whirl and plonk of his line as he cast it into the deeper pools. Every once in a while Frank heard the men shout:

"Slow! Bring it in slow. No, no, let some line go. Shit. Where's that net? Oh, it's a beaut, it's a real beaut. "

Always pretty much the same. Always everything said twice like a demented echo. Gus lifted his head, grunted, "Atta boy, atta boy," when he heard the shouts, then fell asleep again.

Frank fished in a pair of old holey canvas running shoes. His waders leaked and had got too brittle to patch anymore. Couldn't afford new ones, with all the kids, fixing up the basement as the girls' bedroom and, maybe, trying to do a holiday at a cottage this summer, too. Bertha, his oldest, was thirteen and had never had a family vacation away from home. He'd make a go of it if Elizabeth was game. Borrow some money from the Credit Union. Kids and debts, he had plenty of both.

Frank looked over at Gus, whose legs were stretched out like shiny, smooth frogs' legs, spread wide at the crotch, bent at the knee, dappled as the sun shone on them through the leaves of a tree. Gus could've lent Frank his waders. But Gus didn't offer. And Frank never asked. Never would.

Heat built around Frank's head and shoulders. It mixed with the tinny smell of earthworms and water, and the sweetness of bruised grasses at the river side. He let his line fly, listened to the whir and zip as it moved through the air.

Frank took a break to have a smoke and dry out a bit. He imagined that his feet must be like albino prunes. He lit a cigarette and blew the smoke at the blackflies that began to bother him. He held the cigarette in the side of his mouth, squinting through the smoke. He undid his laces, pulled a wet shoe off with a popping whoosh as he broke the suction of water holding the shoe to his bare foot. He tossed the shoe aside and looked at his foot and a wave of faintness passed through him. He took his cigarette, drew on it hard, blew the smoke at his toes. He leaned forward and placed the hot tip onto the leech that lay long, flat and black across the indentations of four of his toes. It sizzled and pulled into itself, lifted off his skin. Frank flicked the leech into the grass. He took another hard drag from the cigarette and touched the second leech that curled over the toenail of his big toe. It too sizzled. He pulled phlegm and bile from his throat into his mouth and spat in the direction he had flicked the leeches.

Frank's toenail was softened and fleshy where the leech had started to dissolve it, sucking for blood. He rubbed it to remove the slime. He finished his cigarette and decided to fish in bare feet, standing in the shady shallows. He could see what was going on with his feet then.

That's how he got the sunburn. He fished the rest of the day barefoot at the edge of the river, his tender white feet exposed to the sun. At five he knew they were burned; by suppertime he couldn't even taste the feed of rainbow trout that Vern fried up in butter. He was too distracted by the cooking of his skin as it swelled and began to blister. When he crawled into his sleeping bag, dizzy from too much rye, the pain remained. In the middle of the night he unzipped his bag, stuck his feet outside because the brush of the soft flannel lining was too much. When it touched the hairs on his toes, his feet twitched with a prickling pain.

FRANK TOSSES HIS SHOES onto his porch and pulls the screen door handle. The hardwood floor in the hallway feels cool. Everyone in the neighbourhood will know the sunburn part of his story soon enough, but the leeches part he'll save for Elizabeth. He'd purposely not told Vern and Cliff about those leeches, and he'd never have told Gus. He'll tell her tonight. In bed. He can hear her groan then begin to laugh at what happened. She'll help him figure out how he is going to get his feet into work boots tomorrow morning. But right now he has to find his screwdriver to unbolt the lock on the bathroom door. It isn't the first time one of the kids has locked themselves in, but with David you never know, you just never know what will happen next.

Frank hears Elizabeth and Vern trying to talk David into unlocking the door. David is crying. Screaming actually. Over this he can hear the sound of water running.

"Turn the water off, David. Listen, sweetheart, do as Mommy says. It's OK. Just turn the water off and open the door."

"How long has the water been running, Elizabeth?"

Elizabeth does not turn to look at Frank but continues to talk to the door handle.

"I don't know. Daddy's here now, David. He'll help you open the door."

Frank bends over and loosens the screws at the sides of the lock. Water is seeping under the door, but not too much. It is cold, and after the first shock is almost pleasant.

"This water is freezing. Are you sure you don't know how long it's been running?"

No one answers. Elizabeth, Vern and Cliff stand back from the door as Frank loosens the last screw. Frank kneels, reaches to grab the door handle as it comes away from the wood and falls into his hands. He sets it on the floor. David is quiet; the water noise is loud. He pulls the door wide and runs straight into his father. He takes one step back, says, "Daddy?" His eyes are dark and look over Frank's shoulder at Elizabeth. He begins screaming again. Frank lifts him straight up holding him at the shoulders. He turns, hands him to Elizabeth.

"Put him in his room. Make him shut up."

Frank sees that David has put the plug in the sink, then turned the water on. Frank pulls the plug and turns the faucet off. Soaking wet towels and the bath mat are wedged along the bottom of the door, which explains why so little water came out that way. Most of the water has run straight down along the bottom edges of the toilet and the bathtub. Frank realizes that it must be gathering in the basement below.

"My room." Frank whispers this.

"My room! The girls' bedroom!" He begins to shout. "Elizabeth, the water. It's going into my brand new room!"

Frank looks at Vern, then Cliff. Elizabeth runs to the bathroom. The three men push past her and run toward the basement.

Vern turns and bumps into Elizabeth who has started to follow.

"I'll get our mop. Cliff, go get yours," Elizabeth says.

They leave. The screen door whaps behind them. Frank limps as fast as he can down the stairs, slams his foot into some pop bottles left on the landing and howls.

"E-LIZ-A-BETH!"

The door to the girls' new bedroom is closed. Two inches of water cover the cement in the rest of the basement. Frank opens the door and a rush of water pours out. By the time it levels there is a three-inch covering of water everywhere. The worst of the flow is coming from the ceiling tiles directly under the bathroom, right over Bertha's bed. Frank pushes the bed out of the way. It is heavy and the bedding is dark and soggy.

Vern and Cliff arrive, wearing their hip waders, carrying scrub mops and pails. Elizabeth, who has been standing at the door, walks into the room in her leather shoes, which spurt a funnel of water up from the instep every time she sets her foot down. She looks around the room, starts to back out, her hands pushed deep into the pockets of her apron.

"Oh, Frank," she says. "Oh poor, poor Frank. Your room. "

Frank watches her until she is gone. He doesn't say another word. Not one. Cliff and Vern begin to mop up, trying to push water out the door toward the drain in the laundry room. Cliff slushes his way out, following the path the water should be taking but isn't.

"It's capped, Frank."

Cliff returns to the bedroom holding the brand new twist-on cap Frank had installed on the drain to stop the kids from sticking Tinkertoys through the holes of the old one, yet allow Elizabeth to open the drain when she needed to do the laundry. Frank only grunts. The water level begins to go down.

Frank presses on one of the soggy white ceiling tiles that he had just finished installing the week before. A perfect white tile twelve inches square, fitting neatly into the tiles that surround it. He pushes until the tile cracks away from its staples. A torrent of water runs down, soaking him. Cliff begins to laugh, but stops abruptly. Frank is not smiling. With the cold water flowing away, Frank's sore bare feet begin to hurt again.

The three men work until most of the water is gone. Damp spots show everywhere. They haul the mattress outside to dry, and Elizabeth hangs the bedding on the line. An audience of children has gathered along the edges of the window well to watch the basement clean-up. They are silent as they watch, run away to giggle in the corner of the yard, and return subdued and grim-faced just like Frank. David has fallen asleep on his bed, Elizabeth reports, when she brings the men some beer to try to lighten things up.

Frank kneels to wipe up one last pool of water. He almost caresses the floor tiles he still hasn't paid for. When the bill is paid, Elizabeth will file it in the ledger in the top drawer of their dresser. Right now the bill is sitting on the kitchen counter waiting for a loan instalment to come through.

Soft lines like sadness appear around Frank's mouth. He remembers coming down to finish wiring the sockets and screw the plates into place. The girls—Bertha, Catherine and Margaret—had been sprawled out on their stomachs, passing a magnifying glass from one to the other.

"What are you doing?"

"We're seeing if this here's real gold, Daddy. If it is, we're rich, aren't we?"

He'd laughed and laughed. "Oh, I wish, girl, I just wish."

The floor tiles are white with clear acrylic pools of floating gold glitter embedded in them. He liked them from the moment he saw them in the building supply store, and so did Elizabeth. The water won't damage them, but all the new wood underneath will take days to dry, maybe weeks.

Frank looks up. Elizabeth is watching from the doorway; Veronica is back on her hip.

"Hope the weather holds."

"Frank?"

"Said, hope the weather holds 'til this is all dried out. Where are the kids?"

"Helen's feeding them hot dogs from the barbecue. She's saving some for you fellows, too. Why don't you go now while they're still warm? I'll help out here."

Elizabeth holds Veronica with one arm and reaches with the other to touch Frank's hand, then lifts it to say good-bye to Cliff and Vern.

"Helen's going to keep the girls tonight, until we get things dried up some. It'll be okay."

"I know. It's just that I only finished Thursday and this is Sunday. It's not even paid for, Elizabeth, and it's wrecked. And look at these feet. How am I supposed to get my boots on and go in to work tomorrow?"

Frank stands looking down at his feet, which are wrinkled along the sides and bright red with blisters that are grossly swollen across the top. Elizabeth looks down at them too. She just shakes her head.

FRANK AND ELIZABETH GO TO BED after midnight. David wouldn't settle down after sleeping in the afternoon. Frank talked to him, told him everything was okay, but never, *ever*, do that again. David started whimpering. Then he wanted to play. Frank was willing. He had a special feeling for David, a combination of aggravation and admiration.

Frank leans over onto his elbow and turns to face Elizabeth. Elizabeth is lying on her back under the sheet. Frank can tell that she's awake. He starts to tell her about the leeches and the sunburn.

"Eliz...."

"Frank, I'm going to see Dr. Ritchie tomorrow. I wanted to wait until after the fishing trip, after the girls' room was finished to tell you."

She turns on her side and faces Frank.

"Are you sure? I thought you had a period last month."

"No. That was just some spotting. Nothing came of it, I'm pretty sure, Frank. In fact, I'm positive."

They lie together facing each other. Their bodies do not touch. Frank sits up and yanks the sheet out from the end of the bed, tucks it around his legs and leaves his feet out. He lies back with a thump. Some of the blisters on his feet have broken. Clear fluid oozes out and dries in patches and crusty dribbles on his skin.

"Good night, Frank."

In all their married life Frank has always kissed Elizabeth good night. Except, that is, when she's in hospital having babies or he is away fishing. Tonight he's not going to do it. He won't make a habit of not kissing her, he knows this already, but just this once he is not going to kiss Elizabeth good night.

He thinks of her nipples, knows their look during pregnancy— large and dark, almost bluish-black. He begins to reach for her. His feet bump together. The pain makes him suck in his breath. Not tonight. Damn it to hell, not tonight. And he won't tell her about the leeches either, maybe not ever, but definitely not now.

Soup's On

ERIN MCNAMARA

EVERY DAY the White Rose served soup.

The stock pot squatted on one of the rear burners of the big gas stove. Into this pot went all the leftovers that were fit for soup. Spaghetti noodles cut up small, sliced carrots and wrinkled peas leftover from the roast beef or turkey dinner specials. Even the leftover meat sauce from Tuesday nights. It all went into this vat and it simmered all day, the level of the pot rising with each addition.

The cook melded it all together by the addition of an industrial-sized can of stewed tomatoes and one of Beef with Vegetables and Barley.

The waitresses ladled out their own cups and bowls of soup into white stoneware with a green stripe.

The lights in the ceiling gleamed wetly and out of focus in the orange grease slicks that gathered on the surface of the soup.

When Maggie plunged the ladle down under the surface, and gave it a good stir, the meaty tasty bits swirled around, and she tried to get as much of the good stuff and as little shine as possible. Sometimes, though, she had to take a paper towel and dip the corner into a pool of grease to suck it up. Then she could serve it to the customers with only a little embarrassment.

Through the swinging doors behind her, the lunch rush was just getting under way.

"Maggie, you got a table."

Bernadette poked her head through the In door.

Maggie let the ladle sink under the peas and barley and wiped her hands on a tea towel.

Two men were seated at a square table for four near one of the front windows looking up the flowered hill to the road.

They were heavyset, ruddy faces peppered with white whiskers, their green work pants pressed. Clean plaid flannel shirts—one in browns, one in blues. A crisp white ring of undershirt shows beneath their collars, a farmer's ascot.

One vinyl-covered menu lay on the table. The blue flannel man held the other upside down before him.

"Jesus, I should know who these people are," thought Maggie as she smiled her best friendly-waitress smile.

"What's your special today, dearrrrr?" asked the blue flannel shirt, with a brisk rub of his nose across the back of his hand.

"*Yellow pepper risotto,*" she thinks.

Yellow pepper risotto, chicken with brie and apples, rabbit with armagnac and prunes. The plates, the endless plates set down before her on sparkling white linen next to cutlery with fiddle-head handles. Around her the swirl of laughter, like vermouth licking around a martini glass cold in her remembered hand so white, with nails so silver. Just enough of the cocktail downed to bring that golden halo to everything around her in the restaurant, to make it all just a bit more vibrant, pushing the whole experience into a heady cloud of smart and fetching possibilities.

She snapped back into her Cape Breton Tartan skirt and white blouse. The men stared. Waiting. For the special. It's the same thing each week, changing daily. Monday is hot roast turkey sandwich with fries. Tuesday is spaghetti with meat sauce. Wednesday is a club sandwich. Thursday is corned beef and cabbage. Friday is fish and chips. Saturday night special is t-bone with baked potato. Sunday is roast turkey dinner.

"Today being Wednesday, it's club sandwich with French fries and cole slaw. $6.95. Coffee and dessert included."

"What's the soup of the day?" asked the brown flannel man, after a dainty sip of water.

"Tomato Beef," she says.

He snorts.

"Jaysus, Michael. We're in here every friggin' week and it's always the same thing. Tomato Beef. That's not the soup of the day, it's the God-damned soup of the year."

He slapped the vinyl-coated menu onto the tabletop.

Maggie saw him suddenly slap his hand on the arse of a brown horse, with a black tail swishing flies away. She remembers him. His name is Albert.

"Soup," said Albert.

"Soup," said Michael.

"And a couple of tea biscuits, dear," said Albert.

She scooped up the menus, placed them on the coffee station and wrote up the order on the carbon pad from her apron pocket.

"Be sure to make Michael and Albert two cheques, Maggie. They get cross if you don't," said Bernadette.

Maggie pushed through the kitchen door. The cook stood at the grill; the apron tied tight around her middle turned her into a huge sausage.

"Well, what do you have for me?" she asked.

"Just some soup and biscuits. I'll do it myself," said Maggie.

She approached the soup pot with two bowls, drove the ladle up and down, making the noodles and carrots and the uniformly diced potatoes of the cheating can of boughten soup float, rise, swim in a greasy salty gorge.

"It ain't *pho*," she whispered, as she filled the bowls.

ON THEIR FIRST window-shopping hand-holding walk all the way home, they went to the Wok In for *pho*.

She thought his name was Antoine then. He had been shooting fashion stills on Queen Street West for an indie magazine. In a littered alley, a model wore a clingy see-through peacock print dress and a rather surly and ugly man lurked behind her. Maggie thought it looked strange and impossibly posed and was shocked to see the finished images. The man's mouth had a quality of waiting to it. Like he could wait forever for the peacock woman in the foreground to give in. All she had seen in the shoot was a skinny girl, an ugly man and dirt.

Antoine had seen incipient sex, voluptuousness, hunger.

On that walk home, Maggie didn't know that part yet. They just walked and looked in windows, at bookstores, sidewalk cafés and funky shoes for $650.

"My friend Simone just bought a pair of those Fluevogs. She wears them teaching Grade 4 math in Scarborough," said Maggie.

"Do you like them?" Antoine asked.

"Well, they're expensive. I don't think I could afford them. I mean Simone's a teacher. She makes good money and has no student loans."

"Do you like them?"

"I know he's really popular. Didn't they wear some of his shoes this afternoon?"

Antoine grabbed both her hands and spun her from the plate glass window. He was laughing.

"I just shot the pictures. It won't offend me if you didn't like Fluevog's shoes. Do you like the shoes? I want to know what you like," he said.

He reached up for her hat, a large milk-chocolate suede hat with black acrylic fur trim around the brim. She and her roommate, Celeste, had gone splits on it at a little millinery shop in the Bloor Village. It looked just like the hat PhD's wear during their ceremonies. Same shape. Different texture. They called the hat The Good Doctor and took turns wearing it. Celeste believed it to have mystical powers. Sex powers. She'd gotten laid every time she wore it.

"Do you like this hat?" he asked.

"I fucking love this hat," she said. She turned to look at her reflection in the window. She saw the wide slouchy suede hat with her hennaed hair curling around the brim and down to her shoulders.

"Well, why can't you just say if you like the fucking shoes?" he said, stepping close behind her to look at his reflection over her shoulder.

She could feel him up the length of her, standing there. Felt how hard his whole body was, his belt buckle at the top of her bum, his thighs aligned with hers. Perfectly.

"God bless this fucking hat," she thought.

"Are you hungry?"

She blushed at that. Exposed her eagerness. She was sure he felt it radiating out from her like hot sticky tentacles.

"Yeah, I'm a little hungry," she said.

"Let's go for *pho*. I know a good place right near here. Come on."

He took her hand. And she was aware of the width of his fingers plaited between hers. They drifted up the sidewalk, and washed gently against store windows until they reached the Wok In.

It was nothing to look at. The door was a regular wooden kitchen door with three tear-shaped little windows in the top. Inside, just five booths filled the tiny space. A man and a woman worked behind an L-shaped counter. He manned two woks. She stood before mounds of sliced vegetables, a small knife in her hand. They smiled at Antoine.

They sat at a booth near the front window.

He walked up to the counter and said, "Two number sixes, please."

They talked about clothes until the soup came. Two huge soup bowls. A mound of noodles in the centre, thinly sliced beef cooked in the broth lay scattered around the noodles. Over all were sprinkled sliced green onions and chopped fresh cilantro.

"Ohmigod, the smell," Maggie sighed.

Antoine picked up the chopsticks and a flat wide china soup spoon with a pattern of blue fish leaping up the curved handle.

"This is how you use a spoon like this," he said, gesturing with the Chinese soup spoon.

"You use the chopsticks and the spoon together. You place bits of whatever you want to eat in the spoon. Some noodles, some meat, you dip it down to get some broth. Then you bring the whole thing up to your mouth and use the chopsticks to push it all in."

Maggie could use chopsticks. One summer in a Chinese restaurant in Sydney taught her that. She placed some noodles in the spoon, a piece of meat with bits of onion and coriander clinging to it. A bit of broth.

Then she bent down and began to shovel and slurp at the same time.

Antoine watched her, laughing.

The broth was light and slightly salty. The beef tender and the fresh herbs and onions shot flashes of green springtime through her mouth.

She raised her head from the bowl, and laughed. Antoine reached over with his thumb and rubbed a drop of broth from the corner of her mouth. He licked his thumb.

"Do you like it?" he asked.

"It is so, so good, Antoine," she said.

"I can make this. My mother makes it a lot and I watched her. My brothers don't cook. But I can. What kind of soup does your mother make?" he asked.

"Well, she used to make this wicked chowder. Clams and cod and whatever we had. And potatoes and onions. Her thing was no fucking cornstarch. Ever. She'd walk out on a restaurant that thickened their chowder with it. I can make her chowder. Almost as good as hers. But there's some flavour. Some strange smell, it's subtle. I don't know what it is. So mine is good, but not as good as hers really," said Maggie.

"If I visited Cape Breton do you think she'd make it for me?" he asked.

Maggie tried to picture his Asian features against the backdrop of the White Rose's insistent tartans. She knew what her mother would say if she said she was bringing home an Asian boyfriend. Same thing she said when she brought home a Jewish one.

"My God, Maggie, you know I don't know how to cook for them people."

"Actually, Antoine, she hasn't made much chowder since she opened her restaurant," she said.

Later they kissed on her front porch under the burnt out light, her back up against the pillar where the blue morning glories would be climbing soon. He tasted salty, beefy, so tasty.

And he left her there hungry, panting slightly, on the step.

MAGGIE TOOK A PAPER TOWEL and wiped the edges of the bowls. She placed a tea biscuit on the edge of each serving plate.

"You better give them two, they get cross if they have to ask for another one. And for God's sake don't nuke them," said Bernadette.

Maggie took one plate in her left hand and balanced the other on the flat of her forearm behind it.

She checked her reflection in the stainless steel of the dishwasher, and wiped away where her prickling eyes had started melting her mascara.

"Two soups, coming up," she said, as she backed out of the swinging doors.

Cave Paintings

ANN-MARIE MACDONALD

WHEN THE ATTIC DOOR finally gave way, James saw this silent portrait: *Death and the Young Mother*. It's an overdone, tasteless, melodramatic painting. A folk painting from a hot culture. Naïve. Grotesque. Authentic.

This is not a gauzy Victorian death scene. No fetishized feminine pallor, no agnostic slant of celestial light, no decorously distraught husband. This portrait is in livid color. A crucified Christ hangs over a metal-framed single bed. On either side of the crucifix are two small pictures: one is of the Virgin Mary exposing her sacred heart aflame, the other is of her son Jesus, his heart likewise exposed and pierced to precious blood by a chain of thorns. They look utterly complaisant, Mother and Son. They have achieved a mutual plateau of exquisite suffering.

On the bed lies the Young Mother. Her eyes are closed. Her blonde-red hair is damp and ratty on the pillow. The sheets are black with blood. The center of her body is ravaged. A plump dark woman who looks much older than thirty-three stands over her. This is the grandmother. She holds two dripping infants trussed by the ankles, one in each hand, like a canny shopper guesstimating the weight of a brace of chickens. The grandmother's face looks straight out from the picture at the viewer.

If this were really a painting, there would also be a demon peering out from under the lid of the hope chest at the foot of the bed, looking to steal the Young Mother's Soul. But he'd be pre-empted by her Guardian Angel waiting in the wings to guide her already departing Soul up to God. The Soul, half in, half out of the tomb of her body, is in very good condition, the hair freshly combed, the nightgown spotless, the face expressionless—the first divine divestiture has taken place, she has sloughed off her personality like an old skin. She won't need it where she's going. Above the crucifix, the wall has dematerialized. Clouds hover. Somewhere within is God, waiting.

But since this is not really a painting but a moment freeze-framed by James's eye, the supernatural elements are, if present, invisible. There is the dead Young Mother, the Grandmother, the Infants, the Icons, the hope chest. What can you do with such a picture? You never want to see it again yet you can't bring yourself to burn it or slash it to dust. You have to keep it.

Put it in the hope chest, James. Yes. That's a good place for it. No one ever rummages in there. This is crazy, of course. You can't stuff a memory of a moment into a real-life hope chest as if it were a family heirloom. But for a second James feels as though that's what he's looking at—an old portrait that he hid in the hope chest many years ago and just stumbled upon again. This temporary confusion is a premonition; it tells him that he will never get over this sight. That it will be as fresh fourteen years from now, the colours not quite dry, just as it is today.

James goes out of the room, but not far. His legs give way and he collapses outside the fallen door, unconscious. He doesn't hear the first cries of the babies inside. The involuntary part of his mind does, though. It is just not conveying the message. It is keeping it on a crumpled piece of paper on the floor of its cave. It is taking a break, admiring its cave painting by the light of the dark.

A few moments later, James's hand shoots out and fastens on Materia's ankle, almost toppling her down the narrow staircase as she leaves the room. James's mouth opens a split second before his eyes. "Where the hell are you going?"

"I'm gonna get the priest."

"No you're not." He's awake now.

"They gonna be baptized."

"No they're not."

"They gotta be baptized."

"No!" James roars.

"You gonna kill them, you gonna kill their souls, you're the devil—"

She's hitting him. Closed fists in his face. If the scissors were handy she wouldn't bother to shut his eyes first—"*Ebn sharmoota, Kesemmak! Ya khereb bEytak, ha Hara deenak!*" If the bayonet were near she would not hesitate. And God would understand. Why didn't she think of this before? Materia too is awake now, after a nineteen-year slumber. She will kill him if she can.

James gets her wrists in a vise grip. His other hand clamps across her mouth. Her eyes roll back. James tells her, "Who's the killer eh?! Who's the killer?! God damn you, God damn you, damn you—" He begins to punctuate the curses by slowly slamming her head into the wall. Her eyes are trying to reason with him, but without the help of words her eyes become a horses' eyes, as mute, as panicked. His tears are flowing now. His lips tripping on salt and snot, his nose bleeding, he's retching out the most agonizing man-sobs, the wall is starting to conform to her skull. This time, however, he hears the tiny cries from inside. Like kittens. He picks up Materia and carries her three flights down to the coal cellar and locks her in. Then he goes for a walk. And many fast drinks, of course. Some of us are just not equipped for suicide. When we're at the bottom, suicide is too creative an act to initiate.

Which leaves little Frances. At the bottom of the attic stairs. Based on her upbringing, and from what she has heard and seen tonight, one thing is clear: The babies up there must be baptized. But she has to be careful. She has to hurry. She mustn't get caught. She stands at the bottom looking up.

The attic room has been a place of absolute peace and quiet for the past many months. Until tonight. Her oldest sister has lain up there not saying anything. Frances and Mercedes have been allowed in to read to her and to bring her trays of food. They have read *Black Beauty, Treasure Island, Bleak House, Jane Eyre, What Katy Did, Little Women* and every story in *The Children's Treasury of Saints and Martyrs*. The two of them decided to look up the hard words next time around, rather than break up the reading aloud. They also got their mother to search out recipes for the invalid food found in *What Katy Did* and *Little Women*. "Blancmange" seems to be the favourite of languishing girls. They never do find out what it is. "White eat." What would that taste like?

Frances knew Kathleen must be very ill because of the huge lump in her stomach. Mercedes told her it was a tumour. "We must pray for her." Together Frances and Mercedes have prayed for Kathleen. They have made a little shrine and given up sweets for as long as it takes her to get well.

So here's Frances at the bottom of the narrow attic staircase. She is almost six. She is not afraid of the dark. Besides, there's a little light coming from that room. And she's not alone. Her big sister, Kathleen, is up there. And so are the babies. The babies, which sound exactly like kittens. Frances is very fond of kittens. She's in her bare feet. She's got her white nightgown on and her hair is in two long French braids. She gets to the landing. She's too small to be on eye level with the new depression in the wall; just as well. But what does it matter, she saw how it got here, and now the child is entering the room and she's going to see everything. She's stepping over the splintered caved-in door with her bare feet.

The difference between Frances and James is that, although she sees a version of the same horrible picture, Frances is young enough to be under the greater influence of the cave mind. It will never forget. But it steals the picture from her voluntary mind—grand theft art—and stows it, canvas side to the cave wall. It has decided, "If we are to continue functioning, we can't have this picture lying around." So Frances sees her sister and, unlike her father, will forget almost immediately, but, like her father, will not get over it.

31

What Frances sees: the gore. The pictures over the bed. The scissors. And the babies, squirming slightly and mewing between Kathleen's legs where they have been wedged for safekeeping until the priest can be dug up. So...the secret contents of Kathleen's tumour, revealed; this gets filed under "Normal" in Frances's mind.

Frances devises a way of carrying both babies: she spreads the front of her white nightie on the bed and places the slippery babies on it. She folds them into the fabric, making a cosy bundle. She cradles her bundle of babies and walks carefully all the way down two flights of stairs with her underpants showing, through the kitchen, out the back door, across the pitch-dark coal clinks in the back yard, until she comes to the bank of the creek. There is one scary thing: the scarecrow in the centre of the garden on the other side of the creek. If toys come alive at midnight, what happens to scarecrows? Frances avoids looking at it. "It's just a thing." But she doesn't want to offend it. She lovingly empties the tiny children onto the grass. It's a nice warm evening.

Frances regrets that she didn't think to rifle the hope chest for the white lace gown and bonnet—the outfit that she, Mercedes and Kathleen were all baptized in. Too late now, there's no time, *I have to get this done before Daddy comes home.*

Frances loves her little niece and nephew already. There is nothing she would not do to make sure their souls are safe. She knows that otherwise they die with Original Sin on them and go to the non-place, Limbo, and become no one for all eternity. Frances has never been up close at a baptism, but she's seen him dip the baby's head into the water. The priest is praying, that's for certain, so Frances must pray too. *Hurry Frances.* Frances makes the sign of the cross, *In nomine padre....* In the name of the Father, the Son and the Holy Ghost. She looks at the wee babies in the skimpy moonlight; "Ladies first." She picks up the girl baby, and shimmies on her bum down the embankment to the creek. She wades to the centre. The water is waist-deep. On wee Frances, that is. Her nightgown puffs and floats on the surface before taking on water and silting down around her legs. She makes the sign of the cross with her thumb on the baby's forehead.

Now's the part where you pray. Frances takes a stab at it: "Dear God, please baptize this baby." And then her favourite prayer from bedtime, "Angel of God, my guardian dear, to whom God's love commits me here, ever this day be at my side, to light, to guard, to rule and guide. Amen." Now's the part where you dip the head in the water. Frances tips the baby carefully towards the water. The little thing is still slick and slips through her hands and sinks. Oh no. Quick! *Hen, rooster, chicken, duck!* Frances plunges down, grabs the baby before it hits the bottom, then breaks the surface clutching it to her body. It's okay. Frances's little heart is beating like a bird in the jaws of a cat, she catches her breath, the baby lets out a tiny holler and the sweetest little sputtering coughs. It's okay, it just swallowed a bit of water, it's okay. It's okay. Frances rocks it gently and sings to it a small song composed then and there, "Baby, baby...baby, ba-by...baby baby." There. At least it's nice and clean now.

Frances crawls up the bank again, lays the girl baby down on the grass, kisses her little hands and head and picks up the boy. She knows that you have to be extra careful with new babies because their heads aren't closed yet. Like a ditch or something along the tip of their skulls. It's called a "soft spot" even though it's in the shape of a line. You can see it stretching along beneath the layer of bluish skin that's draped across it. Frances didn't see it on the girl baby's head because the girl baby has a weirdly dense thatch of black hair. But there it is on the boy baby's feathery pate: a shallow trench dividing his head in half. Frances enters once more the waters of the creek and lightly traces the pale blue fault line in the infant's skull. What if someone just came along and poked their fingers in there, what would happen? He would die. Frances squirms at the thought that just anyone could come along and do that. What if her fingers just went ahead and did that? *Oh no, hurry, you have to get him baptized before it's too late. Before Daddy comes home, or before anyone's fingers can press in his head.*

Frances drops the second baby. Oh no. Quick! *Hen, rooster, chicken*—

"What in God's name are you doing?"

Frances's head jerks up, arresting her plunge. It's Daddy. There's the great upside-down V of his legs towering at the top of the creek embankment. He's got the girl baby in one arm.

"Get the hell out of there!"

He's drunk, otherwise he would never curse in the presence of a child. He reaches down and gets Frances by one arm, easily swinging her up out of the water, her soaked nightgown hanging down past her toes, she could be the Little Mermaid invited at long last onto the good ship *Homo Sapiens*, ready to try out her new feet. Except for the bloodstains.

The water is dark. James doesn't see the child on the creek bed. "No!" Frances screams as he sets her down on the grass. She can't find the words. She can't tell him, telling is not an option, this is like a dream, she's forgotten how to say in waking English, "The other baby is in there, he's going to drown, we have to get him out!" James tosses her ahead, herding her in jerks back towards the house. Frances breaks and runs back. He lurches after her. She reaches the edge of the creek and leaps. Over the top. Splash and plunge. She scrabbles about on the bottom for the baby, her lungs are stinging, in this water she's as blind as the newborn she can't find, she finds him. She breaks the surface for the second time as James arrives back, swaying a little, at the creek's edge. She bundles the baby to her chest; it stirs once and is silent. She stares up at her father and the girl baby. She starts to shiver.

James either says or thinks, "Jesus Christ, Jesus Christ, Jesus Christ." He slides down the bank, takes the child and goes through the useless motions of resuscitation. But it's no use. The boy baby was in the water a good twenty seconds too long. Frances's teeth start to chatter, and she wonders if her black and white candy is still at the bottom of the creek or if it has been washed out to sea.

The Doll Watcher

BEATRICE MACNEIL

CRISSY PREAU'S DOLLS are all porcelain and privileged. They mimic Crissy's fragile state, her droopy eyelids and milky skin. Her pale, pink lips display a row of Chiclet white teeth behind her smile. Crissy bites her lip before she speaks. Before she questions anyone. Bite. "I would like to join the club." Bite, bite. "How many dolls do you need to join the club?" Bite, bite, bite. "Are my dolls pretty enough to join the club?"

Crissy is new in the village of Raven River. The Preaus arrived in September, just in time to lead her down the damp path from their house to the school. Her father is the new bank manager in the village. He is a heavyset man with a thin mustache. Pencil thin, like the awkward drawing of a child. He looked like a man of commerce in a dark cloud of tweed and direct decisions. Her mother is faded the pallor of women who are kept indoors for whatever reasons. She spends her days making matching outfits for their only child and her dolls.

Crissy heard about The Doll Watcher Club in the corner of her Grade Four class. Sparkle Mooney is the president. Nobody voted her in. It was Sparkle's idea to start the club. She told the girls, "I'm gonna be the president, so youse can take it or leave it." Sparkle said she was starting the club so she could keep an eye on the dolls and guard them against neglect and abuse. There are fourteen dolls in the club, seven rubber, four plastic, and three rag dolls are registered.

The three rag dolls, Adam and Eve and Angus, belong to Sparkle. The girls said Sparkle made them herself from an old quilt the Salvation Army gave to her mother. Her father is dead or away. Nobody knows for sure. People said Sparkle's mother loves to drink. Loves to linger and lounge under a cork. Sometimes one or two men stagger into her house on Friday evenings, carrying brown paper bags and stagger back out on Monday mornings, empty-handed. They believe they are carrying moonshine in the bags.

The girls obey Sparkle because they are afraid of her. She is bigger and taller and older than any of the kids in her class. Her eyes, as blue as an old vein, thaw their resistance. Her hair, a white blond, is long and limp and full of tangles. She never wears ribbons or bows to give it colour or contrast. Sparkle's front teeth are broken on an angle like the blade of a saw. She never laughs or cries. The boys are afraid of Sparkle too. They believe she broke her teeth on the arms and legs of people who made fun of her. They whisper to themselves that Sparkle looks like an old doll that was left out in the rain. At twelve years of age, she is already erotic when she lets go of her dolls. She hides the swells under her thin sweaters with her clenched fists.

The Doll Watcher Club is set up in the woods, not too far from Sparkle's house. It is made of two-by-fours stolen from the lumberyard and covered by branches. Keeps trouble out. Sparkle said she borrowed the lumber to give the dolls a respectable meeting place. The meetings are held every Saturday afternoon. The first rule, said Sparkle, was that every doll had to be given a pretty name. Sparkle watches for woolly, tangled hair, scratch marks, dirty faces and hands, wrinkled clothes and sad eyes. These are the omens for punishment handed out by Sparkle.

Sparkle orders the doll mothers to strip their babies for the inspection. Alice Keigan had her doll, Flossy Mae, taken from her for a week because of Flossy Mae's tangled hair. Alice pleaded with Sparkle to give Flossy Mae back to her. But to no avail. Sparkle wrapped Flossy Mae in an old towel and carried her home. Sparkle's rules are very strict. She will not give out any information to the doll mothers about their babies throughout the school week. The doll mothers do not know what happens to their dolls, who have to keep company with the paper-bagged men on weekends. When Flossy Mae was given back to Alice, her head was shaved. "There," said Sparkle, "she'll never be knotted again." Alice kissed her bald baby and rocked her in her arms. That Saturday, Thelma Morgan had her rubber doll, Hughie Dan, taken from her for a week. Sparkle said Hughie Dan had dirty hands and was returned a week later with its hands taped up.

Sparkle invited all the doll mothers and their babies to her birthday party in December. She told Adam and Eve and Angus that it was the season of joy, and that everyone would come and sing Christmas Carols around their little tree.

Sparkle hung two balloons on her gate and waited for her guests with Adam and Eve and Angus wrapped in an old coat. Nobody came. Sparkle burst the balloons with her teeth then went into the house. The girls said they were afraid the cake was made with moonshine. The following Saturday, Sparkle took all the dolls from the doll mothers. She said the dolls' eyes were sad and they needed a party.

Crissy Preau was invited to the Doll Watcher Club before Christmas. Crissy got to play the role of the Virgin Mary in the Christmas pageant, with her doll Cyril as the baby Jesus. Sparkle auditioned for the part with Angus. She wrapped him in a tattered white sheet and made a halo with rabbit wire above his head. Sparkle told Angus, "It is the season for joy and you will be king."

Crissy brought her porcelain doll, Veronica Ivy, to the club. The doll was dressed in a green velvet gown with matching hood. The doll mothers circled Crissy and her doll. They had never seen anything as beautiful as Veronica Ivy before. They ran their small hands along the velvet gown and stroked Veronica Ivy's long blond hair. It too, felt like velvet. Sparkle shouted to the doll mothers to get ready for inspection. They stepped back in silence. Crissy removed Veronica Ivy's coat and folded it neatly. She slipped the doll out of the gown. Veronica Ivy was wearing a starched lace petticoat. It was beautiful enough to be a gown, the doll mothers thought to them-selves. Sparkle watched Crissy as she removed the petticoat and long white bloomers cuffed in lace.

Crissy tried to explain the crack in the porcelain and the red nail polish her mother used to seal the break. "It was Daddy," sobbed Crissy. "It was Daddy who threw Veronica Ivy against the wall." Sparkle's voice shook as she grabbed the doll from Crissy and wrapped Veronica Ivy in an old towel. Sparkle cried as she rocked Veronica Ivy back and forth in her arms. Sobbed quietly as the doll mothers gathered around her and stroked her limp tangled hair, and cried along with her in the season of joy.

Sparkle ordered the doll mothers to leave. Except for Crissy. They filed out of the club one by one. Nobody hesitated or looked back in. Crissy's milky skin was cold and damp like the naked doll in Sparkle's arms. Unraveled from the old towel. Scars and porcelain exposed. Crissy's Chiclet white teeth buried her bottom lip. Blood and sweat swam down her chin. Sparkle's old towel caught the spills. Gently. Crissy watched in silence as Sparkle dressed Veronica Ivy and pulled the velvet hood up over her soft hair.

Crissy's mouth twitched. Bite. "What do I have to do now?" Sparkle's face looked old. Older than Crissy had ever seen it. "Do you have a hiding place in your house?" Sparkle's voice came in whis-pers. The way people speak in the dark, or empty churches, for some reason. Bite. Bite. "What kinda hiding place?" Crissy moaned. "Safe hiding places, Crissy." Sparkle answered slowly and continued to speak. "Small places like attics to hide in." Crissy held out her arms as Sparkle handed her the dressed doll. Bite. "Thank...you, Spar-kle." Bite. Bite.

A Trailing Memory

TERESA O'BRIEN

SWAYING ON THE BACK STEP to the sound of Finkelman's 45s, the music a pulse in the sultry air. Peter's voice soft through the evening whispered her over to him, wine in hand. Laughing as he sang along with Motown.

"Will you still love me tomorrow? Tonight with words unspoken, you say that I'm the only one."

Dancing between the geraniums and potted heliotropes and the musky smell of the early lilies. And later Saturday Night Blues and close on the step under an inky ellipse of sky. Quiet, content. Brief summers in Cape Breton. She had sat with Peter on the swing into the warm nights, neighbouring voices muffled by the hedges and the muggy weight of the air. Mock orange blossoms a burst of fireworks, starry white.

Laughter over the darkness. Hanging onto the ephemeral warmth, not wanting to leave when tomorrow it might all be gone.

On a cold winter morning, she had awakened to the fact that everything had gone, the warmth, the smells, and Peter. Most of all, and forever, Peter.

For months after his death she had walked along the beaches beyond the town. Sliding on the tidal slope of egg-smooth rocks on Glace Bay beach, squelching through coal-dusted kelp and the shale at Schooner Pond. She would climb on to the cliffs, her body curved over stunted junipers melting hollows in the snow. Edging closer and closer to the sea, reaching, haze hanging between. Her mind gently released wandered over the water that swept back and forth between Ireland and Canada. Ireland, the solid ground she had left behind. Wondering about that.

And sometimes she thought of Liz on the other side and what she might be doing. Thinking of her more and more. One o'clock here, it would be five there. Would Liz be walking home from work, carrying an umbrella, having tea in Bewley's, or a gin and tonic somewhere? Memories slipped in and out of her head, a chaos of images in the oily sea. Of Peter and then Liz. Of ships foundering. Bodies lost, strewn on beaches.

Then Emily would take her cold, tired body home, driving past houses lost and vulnerable in the shrunken air of winter, wooden frames fragile in the snow. Behind the walls people arguing, kissing, eating as they waited for the winter to end. Boats in blocks, their smooth bellies at rest in the snow.

The snow melted. Time passed. Days lengthened.

She awakened one May morning to a strong sun shining through the windows, a smell of lilac in the air. She walked outside. The place unfamiliar in the glare, as if the garden and surrounding houses had been rearranged overnight. Habit brought her back inside to pull on a pair of leggings, boots and a sweater. Then she got into her car and drove towards the beach.

The ocean this morning was different too. Emily sat in the car, listening to the world on CBC. The words made no sense. She opened the car door, walked slowly towards the water, feeling light, almost weightless. The air around her neither cold nor warm. A dead air. A sudden call of voices from the water. Not as she imagined they might sound if voices ever would or did call. Not a whisper, but a harsh guttural sound so that for a moment Emily was afraid. The voices louder, more insistent, crying out to her. Running into the water now, cold waves lapping against her thighs, imaginary skirts billowing under her. Her hands fell to smooth the salt hard fabric heavy with the freezing sea. As her knees rose to break the swell, pushing out against the water's weight, a din of voices, drowning bodies wailing, calling in despair.

Then Peter's voice, and then the slightly sharp tone of Liz.

Then all was quiet.

The sun shone on the flat cold slice of water, the moiling sea suddenly calm the way it could be sometimes after a bad gale.

Emily looked down along her body, distorted, wrinkled through the greenness, saw the black leggings held wet against her legs and she wept. She turned away towards the beach, released. It was time to leave. Shivering as she waded out of water frigid from ice melt, she turned her back on the sea of souls that drifted back and forth between Ireland and Canada, hair intertwined with seaweed, fingers lengthening as skin slipped away.

She left the empty beach in a rush to get away, drove back to her house in Glace Bay. She called the first realty company in the yellow pages. Called her children and left messages on their answering machines. And the neighbour who helped with the few animals that were left. Then she booked a flight to London and on to Dublin.

She packed a small bag, spare black tights and a book, then looked about at the years of an accumulated household. A family portrait was taken from its frame, the family looking like pale-eyed pioneers, mouths set in firm lines, hair hanging straight. From the kitchen dresser a twisted, rusting hand cast nail from the old farmhouse in Ireland. Dried mint tied to the nail came away in a shower of leaves and dust that fell on bowls from France, pickled lemons from Egypt, shrivelled clementines from Morocco, a St. Bridget's cross.

Going upstairs one last time she stopped by squares of stained glass window. The panes cast purple and orange light on rocks that lay on the sill. Souvenirs of her walks on Glace Bay beach, a litter of what Peter called "immigrant" rocks. Pieces of chalcedony, bottle green inside with a chalky covering. Mined in England, used as ballast on the coal ships that came to Cape Breton, thrown overboard to empty the holds for coal. Over the years these strangers had tumbled and clawed and crabbed their way to the shore. Emily held the small, dense specimens, weighing them carefully, then chose a smooth sea worn piece with a cool, glassy touch.

There was a photograph of Liz on the mantlepiece, black and white, unframed, a piece of cardboard at the back to stop its curling. Liz, in profile, long curved mouth, a straw hat. Probably taken during their second year in university. Liz loved that photograph, the proud tilt of the head, the wide, Sarah Myles' smile that showed her small, even teeth, the bump on the bridge of her nose from some childhood accident. A photograph that said what Liz wanted it to say. Emily loved the photograph too, wondering now why she had never had it framed. She held the photograph for a moment, tracing her fingertip along the bump, remembering her touch. Separation a breakwater for memories, silt settled neatly behind.

Emily dropped the photograph into her bag knowing that if she waited she may not go at all. She had no idea what would happen at the other end, could not even think that far. Another cliff, no promise of solid ground. The bag was closed, a taxi called. Emily pulled on the door and slammed it shut.

The plane was half empty, stretched legs stealing space. Emily closed her eyes on the darkening sky, turned off the sound track of the film. She thought of the time she had flown to New York to meet Liz. Liz had taken a job there, managing to get in without a green card. Emily's son was a year old. Overwhelmed with motherhood, cleaning, washing—and then a postcard had arrived from Liz.

"Why don't you go? I'll manage alright."

Emily had hesitated and Peter, misunderstanding, had said, "There will always be someone around to give a hand."

And there always would, the hapless, deserted male cared for where bereft women would be assumed to cope.

She had packed a bag with whatever she had that was black, then flew off to meet Liz.

New York was Liz in a black linen dress, Italian sandals, ordering shrimp sandwiches in an Irish pub on Fifth.

Liz had brought her on a bus to Battery Park where they had waited in the bright sunshine for the ferry to Ellis Island. A long line of people, even longer queues on the other side. The heat and the crowds making them cross with each other, Liz's elegant frame a disparaging comment on the sneakered hordes that spilled out from their clothes.

Emily and Liz had escaped, walking into the Great Hall of the Immigration Centre, looking for coolness and peace. They had found themselves lost, the outside world forgotten in this damp high-ceilinged place. The room white-tiled like a vast public lavatory, a lingering smell of disinfectant. Black and white photographs, some seeming scorched by fire, ghosts sliding in and out among the visitors who wandered in the halls. She and Liz slipped quietly along, feeling the suffering weight of ancestors, of difficult decisions drawing them together. The huge windows cast a golden light on the soft down on the back of Liz's arm. Emily's fingers had touched that arm, traced the downy hair in a silent acceptance of loss.

Evening. A Greek restaurant, calamari, lamb, wine. A bar full of leather, fondled feet on laps, a pregnant muggy air, flat sexuality. "Two Remys, ice water on the side," Liz had ordered for both of them. Liz's long smile, slow, the even teeth, signature deep red lipstick. An inadvertent arrogance, leaning forward, her dress dipping, white skin. A rush of excitement. Both knowing that the night had to end in sex. Apart but completely aware of each other. A touch on her inner arm, a finger dipped in brandy and licked.

They stumbled in the door and up the three flights of dark staircase, onto Liz's bed. Cool hands along her thigh, unbuttoning her dress, smoothing the silk of her underwear. The sex intense, a physical wrenching and flesh draining into the folds of itself. The next morning Emily had packed her black clothes, called a taxi and gone back to Canada.

A year later, Liz had phoned. "Just read an article in *The New York Times* about the Cabot Trail, sounds beautiful. May I come for a visit? Can I?"

Rain all day, intermittent cloudbursts, screeching child strapped into a car seat through Margaree and Cheticamp. A stop for biscuits to pacify him. The car stuffy. Liz wondering aloud about sweet biscuits and his teeth. Emily desperately feeding him wine-soaked crusts at dinner, trying to make him sleep, stop his incessant demands. Soothe his anger while Emily had tried to talk to Liz over the din.

That night in the hotel room, the child still cried until Emily lay down on the bed, tucking him alongside her. "Won't that ruin him?" Liz had asked.

"Don't be silly. That's such an old-fashioned notion."

"Oh, well, I wouldn't know anything about that, would I?" And then, "Do you mind if I have a cigarette?"

"No, no, not at all."

The three lay in the dimming light, Liz's cigarette glowing and fading, the child now quiet.

The next morning was fine with a clear view down towards Cape Smokey. They stopped at a long beach. Liz, skirt bunched in one hand above her thighs, walked into the water just beyond reach while the child quietly sifted sand in one of her Italian sandals. With her high arched feet and long fingers, Liz again made Emily feel lumpish and awkward.

The night before Liz left, they sat in the garden at home in Glace Bay. Above them the lights of planes flickered as they tracked between the same two stars of the Plough. Liz swirled the lemon in her drink.

"Well, Emily, it's worked out alright for you, hasn't it?"

"I suppose so."

"You could have chosen a different route, Emily, written a different ending. But you're not a risk taker, are you?"

And Liz got up and went to bed.

Emily sat for a long time then under the birch tree, waiting. Liz did not come back out, the light in her room switched off.

"What are you doing in the dark, love?"

Peter had come out onto the back step.

"Watching the universe."

Running his hand along her neck, he placed two purple roses on her lap.

"Are you coming to bed?"

"No, not yet."

Sitting alone in the dark, her knees drawn to her chest in a spasm of sudden, unexpected pain. The pain gave way to an emptiness, a loneliness, or a just not knowing, or the warmth of the night and the promise. Wondering about growing older and set in one's ways and wanting something else, just wanting. And she had crushed the heads of the roses, the petals bleeding a bruised stain on her hands.

The Christmas card told Emily that Liz was back in Dublin. Emily replied. More cards, another child. Looking Liz up in Dublin. Gin and tonics in the early evening. "Good-bye" and "Keep in touch" and the cards coming only once a year. Then not at all.

Emily covered herself with the airline blanket, closed her eyes but she could not sleep. She was glad when the cabin lights were turned on and the crew started down the aisles with trolleys.

Spilled out into the dawn of London. Four hours lost. The British Midlands flight full, thick with young men and women in suits, cellular phones, briefcases. Caught in the middle seat, a sickening smell of scrambled eggs through the air conditioning. She refused her meal, closed her eyes to the tearing foil that would expose the eggs.

She rented a small red Toyota Starlet in Dublin, adjusted the mirror and slowly pulled out, concentrating so she would remember to drive on the correct side. The road barely wet, the car in front sending skites of mist onto the windscreen. She parked along the Green under a damp umbrella of trees, and walked down Baggot Street looking for a café.

Staring sightlessly through a plate glass window, she tried to remember which street ran off which. Along the canal and out, no, she would have to go through Ranelagh, or was it Rathmines?

Her eyes slowly focussed on the display in front of her, a butcher's shop. The meat laid out in pinkish red slabs on the cold marble, blood oozing over the whiteness, snow covered in blood. A winter when the snow had been deeper than Emily had ever known before, freshly falling it seemed every day. Outside the snow had settled into buckets, barrels and over weeds, firm banks undulating over the fields, covering everything in a blinding, distorting whiteness. She and Peter had walked down to the barn the morning a neighbour had butchered their Highland cow. The immense body a wild orange like a huge felled marmalade cat. Snow covered in blood, warm, seeping into the crystals, fanning outwards, lighter towards the edges, cutting rivulets. And then a long stretch of startling crimson where the slaughtered animal had been chained to a tractor and dragged up the hill to the shed.

In the still, cold evening she had run up the hill along the blood trail, away from Peter. Away from her sudden desire to see her own blood red in the snow.

Now snow muffled the noise of the busy Dublin street. Emily moved forward to wade through the marble snow.

"Oh, for God's sake, Emily!" as she hit her head against the plate glass window, wondering if anyone had noticed and whether they would care. She reached in her bag for the address book and her hand touched the tiny piece of rock. She tightened. It was time to phone.

"Liz, it's Emily."

"Emily!" Silence, then:

"Where are you calling from?"

"A public telephone on Baggot Street."

Quiet. The seconds clicked down on the digital display.

"Could you meet me? Outside Nesbitts."

"Of course." Then: "This is a great surprise. I must say I'm dying to see you."

Emily replaced the receiver as the seconds rushed to zero.

There was a paper stand a few doors down and Emily moved there, her eyes roaming the headlines.

"Two dead in weekend accident." "Body of abducted woman

found, police say still wearing slippers." Emily had the unbidden image of pale, blue mottled legs trailing behind a limp body, plaid slippers or would they have been baby pink with fake fur trim? How had they stayed on the woman's feet when she was dragged from her home? Had she been sitting by the fire, her feet up on a stool, unaware of imminent danger? Emily moved away quickly. She felt vulnerable, nervous. Standing on a busy Dublin street with one bag to her name. The memory of a narrow bed in the front of a redbrick house, dark, rain swept windows and in the half light, reaching over and tracing the ridge on Liz's nose.

Emily waited quietly now.

"Emily? There you are!" Liz called with satisfaction as if she had found Emily out of the blue.

Liz pushed through the crowds, long skirt, black Doc Martens. Emily felt an intense relief. Smiling, Liz's arms reached around her, hair now tinged with grey a sweep across her cheek. The light fragrance.

"You poor thing, you look lost," Liz said as she hugged her.

"I am a bit.... I thought I'd be alright.... Stupid of me, to assume...."

Liz looked mystified but said only, "Well, how are you? You must be tired?" and she tilted her head, surveying Emily.

"Anyway, you look as though you could do with a drink. Come on in here and we'll catch up on things."

Liz reached an arm around Emily's waist, guiding her through the glass doors of the pub into a foetid air of leek soup, cigarettes, beer.

She ordered two gin and tonics.

"Are you home on your own?" Liz asked then.

"Yes, on my own."

"Well it's lovely as always to see you, even if only briefly. I suppose this is the usual flying visit."

"Actually, no." Emily said this quietly, and Liz missed it, searching for something in her handbag.

"And you survived another Canadian winter," Liz said, laughing, reaching over for Emily's hand, holding it just for a second. She took her hand away, stirred her gin and tonic with her finger. A girlish gesture, showing off her elegant hands. Emily glanced at her own hands. Broad, strong.

"My working class hands," Emily would say in her student days. The old desire to hide them was still with her.

"How are the boys? Michael must be what? Twenty-three?"

"He's fine. He's living with a young woman in Quebec City now. They're both artists, paint street scenes to survive."

"Tell me about Peter."

"Peter's dead, Liz. He died three months ago."

Liz reached forward as if to hold Emily, then quickly withdrew. She leaned back to rearrange her scarf.

"Emily, how dreadful, why didn't you write?" Her hand managed to find Emily's again, a brief squeeze and the hand was released.

"I got into the habit of going out to the sea every day. Watching the waves...the water stretching away. Right over to Ireland. I thought that it would guide me in some way." And then with a short laugh: "It sounds a bit ridiculous now."

"No, no, not at all," Liz said, moving away into the silence that lay between them in the hum of the bar, broken by the flick of Liz's lighter.

Emily sat in a fugue, her eyes noting small details. The wood at the end of the bar with brass inlays, a coral sleeve fixed in the groove. Red velvet on the bench shredded at the edges, worn to pink in places. A man, trousers stretched over his wide thighs, his legs splayed, genitals pushing against the grey cloth, the threads on the inseams miniature ladders. An arm ladled soup from a plastic, plug-in tureen. The man with the grey trousers lifting his pint delicately and sucking the top from it. Liz saying again how sorry she was and asking how had he died and what kind of a service had she had and all the time a pink-tipped finger tracing the clasp on her black leather handbag. Emily's fingers purple with the cold the day she buried Peter, or wanted to bury him. The ground frozen so hard, the black shoes left no mark.

Emily told Liz that she had gone for the burial on that sleety morning, had imagined shovels slicing through layers of ice and grime and snow. Thin lines of settled coal dust revealing the weather history of the winter. Instead, the coffin was taken to a stone building for storage until the frost left the ground.

How she had imagined Peter's frozen body slowly thawing, disintegrating, trapped inside the wooden, mushy, splintering coffin. Then the body. Corners missing, rotting, blood blackening in flesh.

How she had ordered the coffin back to the funeral home, insisting on the crematorium while winds whipped her body.

"It must have been very hard."

"It wasn't what he wanted...."

"Still, if that's what felt right...." Liz glanced briefly at the two men beside them.

"I let him down, I think...."

"Of course you didn't. Peter would have wanted what you wanted." Liz said this crisply, picking up her drink.

Emily was not so sure.

"After the cremation, I had the ashes divided and put in boxes. Oval, with mother of pearl on the top. I gave one each to the children. They can...," and she stopped, finding herself trapped in the serene gaze of a woman opposite. Listening, her hands clasped in front of her, her figure wide, flat, one-dimensional, like a cardboard cutout or a pop-up figure in a circus. Waiting to be knocked back, only to spring up again and again.

They can what? she thought. Worship them at night, put them on altars? Bring them to bed? She didn't know. Only ashes, dust.

The pub's warmth sat on her like a blanket.

"And you?" Liz asked gently then, lighting a cigarette, passing it to Emily.

"I don't smoke." But she took it, held it while it burned. Who needed ashes? She remembered Peter's body stretching along hers at night, legs intertwined, bartering cold for warmth between the cotton sheets that felt like silk from too many washings. Small rips trapping toes and hands as they had struggled to consume each other. Her hand clutching a piece of his hair, as if he might drift away from her in the middle of the night. All around them the glow from the streetlight. And sometimes in her dreams the hair she clung to slipped through her fingers and she would awaken to the thought that Liz was with her again.

The ice cubes were melting in the glass. Emily rubbed her breastbone with cold fingers, dispelling the panic.

"I'm not going back."

"You're not going back?"

"The house is for sale, Liz, I'm moving back here, back home." Liz said nothing but she had stopped drawing on her cigarette. Then she stubbed it out into a growing pile of red-smeared butts.

"Emily, do you think that's wise?" she asked calmly. "It seems a bit precipitate." The detached tone in her voice unnerved Emily.

Liz stood up to remove her jacket which she laid on the bench behind, carefully folding it over.

"What about all your things, Emily?"

"I just left them.... It's over."

"After years of living there?" Liz persisted, rearranging herself on the stool. "Do you think that's possible? Just to leave everything behind?"

Emily looked at Liz, wondering how she could explain, wanting not to have to explain anything. She had wished only to close the door behind her, dispossessed. She had hardly dared imagine how Liz would greet her. But in the back of her mind she thought she would be held, she would be told everything would be alright, and now as Liz sipped her drink Emily felt increasingly foolish.

"You're going up to your family then?" Liz asked, dismissing the subject of Emily's house and possessions.

"Yes." Emily had not considered that.

"You should have booked a place here for the night, Emily. Given yourself time to adjust."

"I never thought," Emily said.

Liz raised her eyebrow in assessment. "You look a bit distraught," she said. "Probably jet lag and everything else."

Then the deep breath, "Why don't you stay with me? Just for the evening?"

"You're probably right, Liz. It's not a good idea to drive on now."

THE FLAT WAS SMALL AND BRIGHT, yellow and white everywhere. A pair of half finished yellow chintz curtains lay on a long table beside a sewing machine. Liz's favourite colour, Emily remembered. Remembered too a yellow dress, brown shining hair falling over it.

Photographs on a table, irises in a long glass jar, a piano sonata on the record player—everything neatly arranged, like a shot for the properties section in a newspaper. Nothing to tell a story except the half-sewn curtains and the colour yellow.

Emily took off her shoes and lay down on the sofa. She must have fallen asleep because the sound of the door closing startled her and like a guilty child she threw her feet to the floor and jumped up.

"Sit down and I'll get some wine." Liz returned with a glass. She sat down as if she was going to say something, a hand on Emily's knee. Then she got up, left for the kitchen. The hand a print, a trailing memory. Liz brushing Emily's hair with slow strokes. A coal fire, dying, everyone else in bed. The landlady calling, "Time for bed, girls." Her square figure disappearing into the basement.

"Not yet," Liz had whispered as her brush caught a tangle, separating strands of hair, combing them with her fingers. Then fingers on Emily's neck, Liz's hand pressing down on her shoulder with an urgent insistency, warm breath along her neck and as Emily turned, Liz's mouth on hers. Emily was surprised and not, had noted the taste, the slippery feel of lipstick. She had held back her neck for lower kisses and Liz's hand had slipped under her sweater, along the bare skin of her back. "Come to bed with me," Liz had said. The nights a blur of warmth and desire. Sometimes Emily wasn't sure if it was all a dream. Or indeed if she wanted it to be a dream. Half-awake mornings. "Don't go, Emily, you hate economics anyway, don't go." And the landlady calling, and the smell of bacon.

At the end of that summer, Emily moved out, telling Liz only that she needed her own place. Emily saw less and less of Liz. Then one night she found herself beside Liz in a bar. The memory of Liz's mouth on her breast and the falling in the pit of her stomach and she had stayed, drinking too much. Sins, lack of courage and she ordered more drinks while Liz had gently protested, refused hers. Challenging Liz into what? Forgiveness? Understanding?

Her seventh or eighth pernod, water and ice a milky swirl in the glass. Sick in the toilet. Liz had come in, wiped her face with a wet handkerchief, held Emily while she straightened her clothes. Then Emily's basement flat, cold, damp, a pungent smell of mildew. Clothes heaped on a sofa, dirty dishes in the sink. Liz had looked around and sat on the unmade bed.

"It's easier for you, isn't it, Emily?"

"What's easier?"

"To be with your other friends."

"I don't know what you mean."

"No? Beyond your imagination, isn't it? And you're supposed to be the creative one," Liz had said bitterly.

"Just because I've chosen a different...."

"Chosen?"

"Right!" she had said.

"Right." And she had walked out the door.

The following weekend Emily called Liz. She apologized, then asked to borrow Liz's flat for studying over the weekend. So much warmer, brighter, she had insisted, knowing Liz would be away, would not refuse. She took Peter there, spoiled Liz's bed. Shook out the crinkled sheets and telltale hairs, the crumbs from Liz's mother's porter cake that they had devoured for breakfast. Then closed the door on the weekend and for a long time on Liz.

When she told Liz that she was getting married, it was by card.

Liz had replied, "Delighted. Now you need not commit any more sins."

LIZ DIPPED TWO SLENDER FINGERS into the drink she had poured for herself, squeezing the piece of lemon.

She gave Emily a long look, startling her with a memory of those fingers trailing scratches on her body, drawing imaginary tattoos on her belly. A butterfly today. Or perhaps a python curling round and round? And the nails softly scoring into her flesh.

Liz licked her fingers, turning away.

"We drifted, didn't we, Liz?"

"I suppose you could call it drifting," Liz said, a slight emphasis on "you."

"Well, what would you call it?"

"We might as well use the table, I don't often get the chance."

And she went about setting the table, white napkins on a yellow cloth.

They had pasta with a sauce of lemon and basil. Liz pushed the empty plates aside and lit a cigarette.

Emily sipped her wine, wanting to ask a thousand questions. What had Liz been doing for all these years? Besides the part-time job, the sewing? Who had she sat with late into the nights, whispering, kissing, sharing cigarettes? Was life as she imagined it might be, or was she full of longing for another chance? Did she too have depths of terror ready to erupt at a word, a memory? She wanted to burst through the invisible wall, but as Liz calmly drew on her cigarette, felt herself excluded. She had no idea now what to say.

Liz brought in brandies and pots of coffee and hot milk.

"Are you happy here in Dublin, Liz?"

"Yes, I like it here. The pace suits me. And I'm used to living on my own."

Emily was quiet, fearful of tripping over more words, feeling herself a disruptive presence but needing to ask, to relive part of their time together. The evening slipping away and the brandy warming her belly, drawing her to the edge.

"Do you remember Palmerston Road, Liz?" she asked, and Liz rose, saying, "Yes. I didn't tell you that Mrs. Simmons, our landlady, died last year. It was in the paper. Seemingly she was related to one of the Easter Rising people."

"I never knew. Do you remember how she used to call us in the mornings when we...?"

"Light years away," Liz said quietly. Then: "I think I'll go to bed, Emily. Have you everything you need?"

She made up the sofa in silence while Emily changed in the bathroom into Liz's long white nightgown. When she came back into the living room, Liz straightened, staring at her as though a ghost was suddenly between them.

A fitful sleep, interrupted by dreams photographic in their clarity. A dream of being with Liz, lovers but their lovemaking not working, frantic and unresolved, and they had tried a different bed, and then another and another and finally had decided, flat and tired, that they would just go to sleep.

Sun was shining through the windows when Emily opened her eyes, a smell of toast, coffee, and for a moment she was totally bewildered, startled by the strange surroundings.

Liz came into the room.

"Good morning. Did you sleep alright? It's a nice day, quite warm. Maybe we could go for a walk before you leave." Then Liz added:

"I'll leave you to get dressed."

They walked across from South Circular to the canal, going along the old towpath. A scum of water filled with styrofoam cups and cigarette boxes trapped behind the lock gates. The scum thick and creamy, the way it was sometimes along the shore after a gale, churning with pieces of sulphurous coal dust and leaving Emily longing for the sea.

"I would love to go to the sea, Liz. To Dollymount perhaps, it's quite close."

"I don't know. Although, really, I suppose we could. If you don't mind driving?"

"You never learned to drive, Liz, did you?"

"No, I never felt the need."

They turned off the Clontarf Road, parked and made their way over the sand dunes, away from the Bull Wall, Howth Head a dark hump in the distance. Emily took off her shoes and rolled down her tights, wading into the water. Liz stayed on shore, just above the tide mark.

She moved further out, hearing Liz's voice calling to her to come back mingling with the sound of the sea.

She kept walking, deeper and deeper, the water submerging her, submerging the memories.

A big wave swept towards her, breaking at her knees, wetting her to the waist.

"Emily! Emily!" and Emily turned to the voice, Liz's body a thin silhouette on the shore, her arms folded around her waist.

"Come back, Emily. Please." Liz called something else but her words were carried away on the rising wind and Emily turned from her.

Another step out, and then another, the waves sucking and releasing.

The sandpipers flew over the water again, miniature planes, swooping flashes of white in trick manoeuvres. The air full of the pips and cherks and wheeps of birds calling and the lonely haunting cries of curlews.

"Emily, you are behaving like a child, you are not twenty years old anymore, please come back."

Twenty years old, how bizarre and unreal it had all seemed, living with one man, setting up a home, and how all that had become her reality. Days of living, the meals shared, the small talk, the getting up and going to work and arguing over no clean towels and wasting money. And all the time opening up and offering their vulnerabilities for safekeeping with one another.

Emily bent forward, dipping her face into the water, opening her eyes to the sting of salt, the swirling grains of sand.

She came up for air, her skin tight, fresh. She wiped the water away, feeling beneath her fingers the lines and hollows of her face, thought, "Duplicitous marks of wisdom."

The water moved past her in long, smooth waves towards the shore and in the other direction, miles and miles of ocean, out to the Isle of Man and beyond, to Liverpool and Holyhead, across Europe and Asia and finally Canada and her own coast, her own water, the beaches waved with fine, shining coal dust. The water blue, and the red and yellow boats weaving around the rocks, men pulling up fluorescent lobster pot markers. The world like Emily's life stretching backwards and forwards. Remembered for a short time, then lost.

Emily turned for the beach, the cold water shriveling her body. The pipers swooped brown, white, brown, white, swoop, swoop.

Liz had moved towards the car.

Emily reached a hand towards Liz, but Liz moved away from the wet, dripping body.

"You're soaked Emily, you look like a drowned rat."

Emily stepped forward, her arms catching Liz, circling her in an awkward embrace. The body in Emily's arms small, fragile. She thought she might crush it. For a brief moment, there was an answering embrace, a tightening of the arms, a cheek laid against her own, a clammy stickiness. Then Liz pulled away.

"I'm sorry, Liz. I didn't mean to scare you." But Liz was walking away, lighting a cigarette. Emily reached for the package on the seat, lit one for herself, drawing in until the end was glowing red. She took a second drag, the inhaled smoke making her light-headed, sending her soaring with the sandpipers.

Emily got into the car and turned the key, the heater on full, the still cold air blasting over her. Seawater soaking the upholstery. She turned the heater off, drew on the cigarette again, then tossed it away.

The sun was high over the dunes, Liz's figure a black cutout against the bleached sand.

The sandpipers made a last swoop and were gone, out to sea, round white bellies skimming the surface and then in unison, they dipped their wings in farewell.

They drove back to the flat in silence, Emily every so often shuddering uncontrollably.

"Look, Emily, you're obviously still in a state of shock," Liz said as she opened the door. "You'd better stay another night." And she set about running a bath and making tea.

"I need to do some work on these curtains. You'll have to take my bed for tonight."

"Sorry, Liz."

"Oh, it's not a big deal."

The sheets felt cool and there was a comforting smell of Liz's perfume on the pillow. Exhausted, Emily fell into a deep sleep, awakening suddenly to darkness, not knowing what time it was. She was keenly aware of herself alone in Liz's bed. And of Liz in the other room.

Emily slipped out of the bed, towards the nightlight beside the sofa. Liz's body curled under a blanket, small and vulnerable, her head back, mouth slightly open. Emily pulled off the long nightgown, then lifted the blanket aside and edged in beside Liz.

Liz opened her eyes and looked at her. There was the sound of an ambulance outside. Flashes of light through the window. Broad rods of light across the room. Liz stared at the lights, then she turned to Emily.

"Emily, what do you want?"

Available Exits

ELLEN FRITH

All tragedies are finished by a death....
Lord Byron

BELLE PITT, 33, committed suicide in the cemetery. It was a clever move because she died among the only non-judgmental group in town. Shannon Falls' already-dead with their rigid tongues and sewn-together lips, and ancient empty mouths, reliably withheld comment on Belle's actions. None uttered a word, nor did they gasp, nor clack yellowed mandibles in disapproval when she sat down one afternoon in late November, leaned back against a headstone of somebody else's grave, and slit her wrists. And as she bled herself white on the grass of that old tomb, her requiem was silence.

For seven days and nights, Belle sat in this boneyard haven, the frost layering a veil, crystal by crystal, across her body, and her face with its faraway smile. While, around her, Shannon Falls dismissed its absent citizen with a shrug. Belle Pitt often disappeared for a few days. People said, "Well, this is just like our Belle. She's off again, you know, on one of her 'travels'...."

Graves and secrets complement each other and Belle might have sat in peace until the spring but for Little R. Although the twelve-year-old girl had pledged to herself to "zipper her mouth and cross her heart and point to God and never tell where Belle lay," the secret proved too mighty. It smote her like an Old Testament God and she lay bedridden, eyes swollen shut, throat on fire, body burning up with fever, the knowledge of Belle's whereabouts clawing at her gullet.

BELLE HAD CHOSEN TO DIE in Shannon Falls' Protestant cemetery, across the main road from the town's Catholic dead. Marshy, bordered by chokecherry trees and scrub alder, the back end of this apostate burial place was south of the town, down beside the river and the railway tracks. Its ground squished with water during the summer and froze solid with the first cold temperatures.

Little R had told Belle that she often played among its plain, square stones.

"The ghosts in that place greet me like puppies and dance around my feet," Little R said, and Belle had nodded.

"I know," she said. "I understand spirits."

"And when I dance there my hair stands on end." Little R twirled around the room demonstrating her steps.

"Of course. They're playing with you. Spirits stay young no matter how old the bodies get. Spirits stay young always...."

"And when I laugh, I open my mouth really wide and the ghosts suck my breath out of my lungs until I fall down!" Little R bounced off the floor, her limbs like rubber.

Belle smiled at her antics.

"Ask those spirits for a gift one day. A gift, nothing specific and you might get it. They might give you more energy to dance for example!" Belle stood up and joined Little R in twirling around the room, her limbs awkward and without rhythm. When she stopped, breathless, she said, "Don't mistake ghosts for angels, though. Angels are grown-up type spirits. They seldom play."

When Little R saw Belle sitting in the cemetery that November afternoon, she thought Belle was playing one of their games.

"Hey!" she cried. She moved forward slowly, placing her feet to avoid tromping on any grass growing directly over where a coffin might be.

According to Little R's sister Rose, avoiding this "blanket" laid over the dead conveyed respect for the departed. And since Rose levied her rules and regulations with the authority of a twenty-one-year seniority over Little R, she was seldom questioned or challenged.

Little R called again, "Hey! Belle!" But when close enough to see the details of Belle's clothing, she stopped, puzzled, one foot still held aloft. Late November was no time to defy the cold and yet Belle appeared to be wearing her traveling clothes. No coat, no boots, just her outfit of skirt, shirt, and Tilley hat bought through an outfitters catalogue. "For my safari to Africa," she had explained to Little R, when it arrived through the post.

Shaking out the khaki clothing from the parcel they had come in, she had hung them prominently in her wardrobe, front and centre.

"Hey!" Little R lowered her foot. She suddenly forgot to be careful of the dead and marched forward, crushing bones, to stand beside Belle.

Belle sat, her long legs stretched out along the ground in front of her, crossed at the ankles. Her traveling shoes—sturdy leather walkers—had been placed beside her, on top of the backpack she always carried. Bared of all but nylon stockings, the skin on her legs had erupted in goose bumps pushing the dark hairs along her shins through the stockings' weave. Little R noticed all this, moving her focus along from Belle's bare feet until it was riveted by the crimson spectacle in Belle's lap. In that immeasurably short time between curiosity and panic, Little R wondered why Belle was wearing red gloves and that silly, little, red, hostess apron. And then she screamed.

The skin of Belle's forearms gaped, four long slices through the delicate cover of the inside of her arm from her elbow to her wrist. Her hands lay palms up upon her thighs, her fingers curled. A straight razor lay closed and tossed aside.

THE IMPRISONED TRUTH about Belle's whereabouts finally escaped Little R when Belle's lover, Jack Black, approached the sick girl's bedside. Although Little R had to rub her eyes often to dispel the image of Belle and Jack in bed together—at twelve years old, she did not yet share Belle's enthusiasm for sex—she liked Jack well enough and thought him "cute enough" with his long face and black beard. A few men in Shannon Falls sported mustaches, but none let all the hair on their faces grow as Jack did. He claimed his beard, unusually silky and flyaway, discouraged germs from invading his body through his mouth and nose. And it filtered the air, he said, purifying it of the mill town's pollution. And the tufts of whiskers that curled up over his ears...well, they prevented him from hearing what he shouldn't.

It was Rose who had called for Jack to attend her little sister's bedside.

At first he had argued that he was too busy looking for Belle to devote time to Little R, but Rose had insisted. Little R was sick and was asking for him, Rose said, and because she didn't like Jack, she added that why, she couldn't guess.

Lowering himself awkwardly, not knowing exactly where to sit, Jack perched himself on the edge of Little R's bed. A grub-shape of blankets ending at the top in a tangle of brown hair indicated where the sick girl lay.

"Little R, it's me. Jack," he whispered. Plucking at the blankets, he found an edge and pulled, uncovering Little R's flushed and feverish face.

Her look of anguish—Belle's secret like a demon pinching her features tight and drawing back her lips until they cracked—caused Jack to suck in his breath.

JACK SAID HIS CONTRIBUTION to Shannon Falls' folkways— it being an English/French town in a bifurcated province—was to preside as its man of opinion, its political pundit, its poet: drawing and glueing the edges of its divide together with good sense. He talked like that, as if words were harriers in a sport, pounding a track of ideas. Lapping his listeners, leaving them in the dust, Jack bamboozled people. When he ran for mayor against Cecile LaVenture, she stated that Jack was a man capable of brainwashing, and the voters recognized the truth. He lost the election, proving his theory "of the inclination towards mass hysteria in the face of superstition, that held sway in small, working-class towns." Later Jack admitted to voting for Cecile himself.

In Belle, Jack had recognized an ally. She matched him, not in verbal skill or cerebral acuity, but in her ability to manage reality with imagination. While Jack could, and often did, view the world through his own pink glasses of wordplay, Belle breathed make-believe like oxygen. In Jack's own words, they broke bread baked of myth and fantasy together.

Belle had once told Little R that, with his vocabulary, Jack could weave a sentence to indicate his horniness into satin sheets already warmed by their bodies. Overhearing Belle's remark, Jack had laughed, Ha! And winking at Little R, his smile split the dark mass of hair that was his lower face. If his nose had not been so full, his nostrils so generous, Jack would have been a handsome man.

HE COULD NOT GO to the cemetery alone. He was too afraid that Little R might be telling the truth. Although he doubted it. The girl was sick after all, and had been known to tease in the past. Of course, even Little R wouldn't tease about something like this. Or would she? Jack didn't know what to do. But since the implications of Little R's story vanquished his common sense, he didn't call the police.

Belle and Jack had once talked of death. Or at least Jack had talked. Belle had stretched out, her head upon his chest, and let the rumble of his words lull her to sleep. As with other subjects, Jack mixed hyperbole with fact and fancy . He talked of the physical reality of death; of death's spiritual significance; of death as merely an end of living; etc., until Belle's snoring disrupted his train of thought.

For her part, Belle simply said that since her entire life was a figment of her own imagination, when she died, her soul would sashay around checking up on everybody. "I'll come back to spook you, my love," she had told Jack, widening her eyes and curling her fingers into claws. "Boo!"

Well, she was spooking him. Already. He could not go alone to weep at the side of his dead love as Little R had begged him to. First of all, he didn't believe Belle was dead, that she could have died without his feeling something. They were lovers after all. And then there was the cemetery, now a November-bleak place of frozen earth and ashes and decay. The thought of traipsing around there frightened him.

Ashamed of this cowardice, Jack called himself a poof and a lily-livered swine. Still he could not go alone. He decided to confer with Cecile LaVenture, the town's mayor, and a woman afraid of nothing.

Cecile stood big-boned, broad of beam and solid. She was near to six feet tall and she yet possessed the centre of gravity of a much shorter person. No one had ever known her to stumble or lose her balance and, as a young women, she had downhill skied with a man's abandon.

"Get to the point!" Cecile said as Jack stood on her doorstep, trembling and stuttering. "What is it? News of Belle?"

Jack nodded. "Little R says Belle's dead in the cemetery." And thinking that this news might disturb even Cecile's dense, atomic power, he reached forward to hug her. She slapped his arms away.

"That's ridiculous," she stated. "Little R's sick and delirious. She's making it up."

But Cecile agreed that the situation required investigation. Taking charge, she said that she would accompany Jack to the cemetery, but first they must tell Osborne Pitt. Osborne was, after all, Belle's husband, said Cecile, withering Jack with a look.

While Jack waited anxiously, Cecile dressed herself up warmly to go out into the dropping temperatures of the late afternoon.

Twenty-five years separated Osborne Pitt from his wife Belle in age, but their constitutions were a century apart. During the ten years of their marriage, he had matched her exuberance with torpor, her physical gaiety with a woebegone stiffness. Now when confronted by Jack and Cecile and informed of Little R's news, he nodded his head and it wobbled on his strengthless neck. He'd been weeping since Belle left and wiping away those tears all week had left Osborne's sad old face raw and gray.

Sighing, he pushed his arms through the sleeves of his winter coat and led Jack and Cecile out the door. The trio moved slowly towards the cemetery, Osborne setting a feeble pace.

"I don't think Belle's there at all," he said, holding tightly to Jack's arm and leaning into the younger man.

Jack nodded.

"But if she's there at all, she's dancing between the headstones, eh?" he whispered.

Cecile agreed with Osborne. It was a waste of time, she said loudly, because Little R was delirious with fever and didn't even know what she was saying.

"Your harebrained wife has simply gone traveling a little farther than usual, but we'll find her," she said.

BELLE PITT SPOKE BRAVELY of the world beyond Shannon Falls as if it was as familiar to her as the lines on her own hand. She said she wanted to explore the last of the earth's secret places.

She wanted to step on ground that was sacred to the gods.

She wanted to breathe air thick with ambrosia and feel the wind like the song of a thousand angels against her cheeks.

She wanted her soul to dance.

She wanted to hold her head in the clouds.

She wanted to tiptoe across the oceans, jumping the waves.

But Belle lacked courage. An inventory of fears wrapped itself around her ankle like a ball and chain. She rarely left her house. And when Belle went "traveling," she disappeared into her bedroom where she locked the door and spent days leaving town by way of a Valium-induced sleep between bouts of hysteria. Sometimes she'd sit and thump the floor with the steady beat of a train's wheel turning until her hands bled.

Very rarely, and laughing loudly at her own courage, Belle boarded the bus on Main Street in front of Chez Pitou restaurant and went to Sherbrooke.

Osborne would finish his shift at the mill and drive up to fetch her. He'd find her sitting on a bench in the bus terminal, snapping her ticket back and forth across her knuckles and swirling her feet in tight circles through the cigarette butts and empty chip packages on the floor.

Osborne said that picking up Belle from Sherbrooke was like rescuing a lost little girl. Belle hissed angrily at these words, stating how could she be lost when she knew exactly where she was—in stinking purgatory!

Sherbrooke was only the first stage of her journey, Belle told Little R.

One day she'd go farther. And where would she go on that day, Little R prompted. "To the earth's secret places," Belle whispered, but she wept, tissues clumped in her hands. "And when I go, it won't be some cheap bargain getaway!"

Naturally the whole town made fun of Belle's travels, some in a kindly way, some not. Little R's sister Rose, who vacationed annually in Florida, laughed that Belle was too chicken shit to go anywhere. But Jack said simply that although Belle's stride was the walk of the traveler, she moved in baby steps. It was just a matter of time, he assured everyone, before she moved on.

SINCE LITTLE R HAD CROAKED simply "cemetery," Jack couldn't say if she had meant the Catholic or Protestant side. They began their search at the far end of the Catholic cemetery, wandering around the headstones, staying in a group, as Jack insisted. By the time they found Belle in her spot by the railway tracks, the sun was low in the sky, the headstones around them casting long shadows across the frosted ground.

First came confusion, then disbelief and shouts of horror, and then Cecile, Jack and Osborne lined up like sentinels beside Belle's body. They stood staring down at her, gagged by astonishment. Jack's mouth hung open so wide his black beard brushed his chest, and, wide-eyed, Cecile breathed with a ferocity that shot twin columns of mist three feet out from her nostrils.

Osborne trembled and whined, and the sun set deeper in the sky.

But unlike the dead of Shannon Falls who, after witnessing Belle's demise in silence, had remained so, the trio of still-animated citizens soon found their voices.

"Jesus Christ! Who the hell would kill themselves in a cemetery!" Cecile bellowed, her voice cracking out from the mist around her face like God from a cloud.

Howling, she raised clenched fists above her head and threatened the sky.

Cecile had loved Belle with a mother's love, but her emotional repertoire was limited. She served up her sadness as wrath. "God damn the girl!"

Cecile expressed other negative feelings as either anger, petulance or rancor, and her happy ones with a self-satisfied smirk.

She pointed an indignant finger at Belle, and forgetting that it had taken them two hours to find her, and that it was the end of November, she screamed, "Look at her! People could have tripped over her, propped up against that headstone like that! Imagine, families coming to the cemetery to pay their respects and what do they find...a dead body!"

Belle had once described Cecile as a volcano—"lava! lava! lava!"—and she was now erupting.

"And why did she pick the end of November to die! Suicides think about killing themselves their whole lives. It's always hari-kari this or hari-kari that! She could have gone anytime! But no, she picks the coldest day!"

To prove her point, Cecile slapped her arms vigorously around her body, huffing indignantly .

"Why? Why now? Her soul's gone—God knows where—but look at her body! Preserved for the whole town to see! Dirty laundry in public."

Spreading her hands wide, the sleeves of her coats lifting, revealing thick, strong wrists, Cecile appealed to Jack and Osborne.

"Why? WHY?"

Jack stood silent. Stunned. While gawking at Belle's body, odd emotions had emulsified his guts. Death had transformed Belle, calming her gawky awkwardness to elegance. It had rounded her long, skinny limbs, smoothed her wayward hair. Her head was tipped gracefully, her chin forward as if she was a queen saying hello, welcoming her subjects. And her blood had flown like honey from her veins: it lay, a pool of sweetness, in her lap. Nectar, thought Jack, the word horrifying him as it leapt to mind. And ambrosia.

He experienced a lust at that moment so crude and ferocious it forced a groan from his throat. If Cecile had not tugged at his sleeve, tipping him over into the solidity of her arms, he was sure he would have thrown himself upon Belle's body. Mortified, he buried his face in Cecile's shoulder and sobbed. Cecile held tight. She thumped his back as if his crying was a coughing spell. Osborne reached out, found Jack's hand, and held it in his own.

The sun had almost set when the trio drew apart.

"She looks still alive," Cecile said, calmer, indicating Belle with a jerk of her chin.

It was true. With the low sun rays pinking the frost on Belle's cheek, and twinkling off the ice crystals in her open blue eyes, it seemed at that moment she might smile, laugh, shake off the game.

Cecile raised her fists to heaven once more.

"WHY?" she roared for the third time.

"Why indeed," said Jack Black. He had regained an element of self-control, his demons retreating. "Why indeed." He straightened his back and reached his arm around Cecile's broad shoulders. "Belle is sitting here in a chilly fare-thee-well to Shannon Falls."

Opposite the road from the Protestant Cemetery with its plots delineated by plain hunks of granite, lay the town's Catholic dead. Roomier by a couple of acres, the Catholic cemetery held bigger, more ornate stones, and the graves were shaded by elegant maples.

"If it was me," Cecile said suddenly, breaking away from Jack, "if it was me, I'd have died in the Catholic cemetery." Digging into her coat pocket, she withdrew a man's white handkerchief. Before blowing her nose, she waved it towards the road. "I'd have died over there."

Jack shook his head. "Killing yourself is more of a sin on the Catholic side," he said. A self-professed reasonable man, Jack claimed that religion interested him more than it inspired, but that you could never be too careful. Surreptitiously he jiggled his right index finger through a modified sign of the cross, a habit he'd developed in school to hedge his bets. Forgive me my appalling lust, he prayed.

Osborne's thin voice, heavy with a mid-European accent, broke in. "More of a sin, less of a sin, it doesn't matter. Belle was never baptized."

"What did he say?" said Cecile. She liked to pretend Osborne's speech was indecipherable. Honking into her handkerchief, once, twice, she cleared her nose. "We'd have seen her sooner over on the Catholic side." She sighed. "Besides it's nicer."

It was no secret that when the time came, Cecile wanted a ten-foot granite angel over her grave.

Jack pulled his own hankie from his pocket and cleared his nose carefully, wiping one nostril and then the other. Folding the hankie in on itself, he replaced it in his coat. Then Osborne produced an old, shredded paper towel from his pocket and blew into that. But he had neither tears nor mucus left for Belle, and his honk was barren.

The trio milled around for a while, studying the sky, the sunset, the tops of the trees, anything but Belle's body on the ground. Jack stamped his booted feet. The frozen ground rang hollow and he wondered how it could considering all the bones and rot and ash it contained.

"The frozen earth is ringing a requiem for Belle," Jack said, stamping again. "It's a cold day for dying."

Impatiently, Cecile moved away from Jack's side. She had noticed Belle's bare feet.

"Forget your requiems, Mr. Poet!" she said sarcastically. "Belle didn't die today. Look at her! Look at her feet!"

Reluctantly Jack lowered his gaze. He didn't like Belle's feet which were large and bony, hanging off her thin ankles like a scuba-diver's flippers.

And because she was vain, she had always worn too-small shoes. The pressure had pushed her big toes into awkward angles, forcing the adjacent digit to flip over like crossed fingers. Belle had laughed at her toes—said they brought her good luck—but they had repelled Jack, a fact he was ashamed to recognize. Instead he dismissed Belle's feet as he dismissed his own nose, as miserable failures in the gene-pool kitchen.

He looked at them now, noticing that her nylon stockings bagged around her ankles and that the tiny dark hairs along her shins poked through the weave.

"I know, her toes..." he murmured, embarrassed that she could no longer hide them.

"Not her toes!" Cecile said, shaking Jack's arm and pointing again to Belle's feet. "She's not wearing shoes! Where are her shoes?"

With little difficulty for someone of her size, she lowered herself to one knee and leant closer to Belle's feet.

"Is that nail polish?" Cecile said, honestly astonished. "What's the point of painting crippled toes?"

"Never mind the nail polish," Jack said. "For God's sake!" He hauled Cecile back to her feet. "Where are Belle's shoes!"

Searching the ground to their right and then to their left, Jack and Cecile walked around the immediate area. It was getting darker and darker.

"And wait a second, where's her backpack? She never goes anywhere without her backpack." Cecile placed her gloved finger against her lips, and looked puzzled, her eyebrows drawn down into a dark V. When she and Jack had returned to their original positions beside Osborne, she shook her head and said, "Something funny's going on here." And then, "Polish on her toenails, I can't believe it."

Suddenly the setting sun dropped from the sky completely and it was dark, the only light source a gray glow from a streetlight on the road. A gust of cold wind agitated the loose edges of the autumn leaves frozen to the grass. An alder branch cracked in the cold.

"What's that noise!" Cecile jumped, startled, her hand against her breast.

"Nothing!" Jack said, although equally alarmed. And then to ease the tension he added fatuously, "Well, maybe it's hell slamming shut."

Osborne swung around towards them, his eyes wide, glaring out from the shadows of his face.

"Will you two shut up!" he cried, hoarse with rage. "She's dead for Christ sakes!"

Growling, his fists cocked, Osborne swung his leg back and drilled the rigor-mortised mass of Belle's crossed feet with his heavy boot.

"Frigging dead!"

The impact of his kick cracked the frost layer over Belle and it puffed up around her, tinkling off in the dim light like a snow cloud in an animated movie. Cecile and Jack stood stupefied by Osborne's sudden violence. They stared at him like deer in headlights. But as quickly as it had ignited him, Osborne's anger dissipated. He dropped his arms.

"Dead!" he said, his voice a whimper.

"My God, you've gone mad!" Jack cried.

In the same instant, Cecile reached around him for Osborne's throat.

"I'm going to kill you!" she roared.

Caught between Osborne and Cecile, Jack struggled to keep them apart.

"Stop!" he cried, his voice shrieking across the darkened cemetery.

"Cecile! Osborne! Stop! Consider your actions! Remember where we are!"

Cecile grabbed a handful of Osborne's collar and jerked him forward, his forehead cracking against Jack's chin.

"I didn't mean it! I didn't mean it! It was just a twitch!" Osborne screamed, throwing himself backwards, away from Jack, his arms flailing, but Cecile held firm. She jerked him up against Jack again.

"This is a twitch, you son-of-a-bitch!" she cried. And lashing out with her foot, she knocked his leg out from under him. He fell, dragging both Jack and Cecile with him. They landed, a struggling mass, so near the dead woman that they thought they could smell her perfume and her blood. It brought them to their senses.

They were just lying there when the Shannon Falls police arrived.

*A*nd *I*f by *C*hance...

KIM WILLIAMSON

*A*ND IF BY CHANCE she could slip through a passing shadow, melt like paper into a flame, evaporate, vanish, she would. She was passing time, knitting socks by the fire, waiting and listening for news of Godo. Shooting past her youth. Red wind, black hash, Springsteen albums, a borrowed summer cottage. A time when all she had to do was relax under the moon by a fire licking and crackling. Yesterday.

Hitchhiking across the border, then west to B.C. where he'd married, was the last news she'd heard. A month ago a friend mentioned he'd opened a shop downtown. She'd seen it and found him.

He'd aged gracefully, slim, still looking like the twenty-three-year-old she'd known. No gray. His blonde hair had darkened. And a tattoo appeared under his shirt sleeve each time he gestured with his arms.

She laughed when he passed her lit cigarettes, leaning back against his desk, still talking. Then invitations to supper. For the next month she cooked.

Then why, she wondered, do people run into each other again? Reason? Chance? Moments like these had no explanations. God was curious, God was funny, but God wasn't stupid.

They talked, walked (for neither owned a car), drank wine, and listened to the Blues in her apartment. For a while it was entertaining. Conversations challenging and nights ending with something as close to making love as she'd ever come.

Two weeks, three and then four, and she could do no wrong. Beautiful, lovely, gorgeous...everything she did was complimented. She wondered why her passion was slowly wearing away when everything seemed so nice. What seemed vital rolled off her tongue like a log dumped from a truck. Her power of speech diminishing within. She had nothing left to say.

Then he asked, "Do you want me to leave?"

"Yes."

"Yes."

"Yes."

She did and he did, leaving the door wide open for her.

She crossed the road, went behind a building and up the back street so as to avoid his shop. Couldn't see him or face him yet. Hallmark cards beckoned her sentiments. Explanations for how and why she felt the way she did, or the sorry.

Sunset after sunset she sat on her balcony cooling down into Fall. Umbrellas and rain, pretending to be in New York or Toronto. A maze of streets crawling with cats and phantom dogs mysteriously shitting on sidewalks. Back and forth, through and around she roamed until she found a new home. A hideaway.

Lavender, to mask the marijuana she was burning, smoldered in a heated pan at the top of the stairs. The aroma of curried vegetables lay in wait for her ravenous appetite. She sipped red wine and watched the wind twist and bend eighty-year-old limbs at will. To be so wild and yet so rooted, she sighed.

The Hallmark moments had passed. No longer did she feel the desire to please or fade away. Imperfection was restored.

Every Girl Turns into Her Mother

JEAN MCNEIL

"CUBA?" I said, rubbing the sleep out of my eyes. "Where's that?"

"Some communist country somewhere," Grandma said.

I had just woken up. My mother was gone.

"Will she come back?"

"I don't know." Grandma slumped in her chair. "She's gone off with.... Well, she's gone off. She left me a note."

"Let me see...." I was getting desperate.

"You're not to see it."

Cuba. I knew a little about it. I knew it was once a place where people were in chains and forced to cut sugarcane from morning to night watched by fat men in white suits who sat on the verandas of grand houses and smoked cigars and drank rum. Sometimes I would see a tourist poster for a place named Cuba. I knew it was communist now, even though they had beaches and bars there, even though communist countries were normally places where people lived in concrete block cells called apartments and couldn't own cars and had to line up for everything they bought and where it was always winter.

"CUBA," I said to Mr. Kapuscinski, my geography teacher.

"Ah yes," he beamed, very pleased that I should be curious about this part of the globe. He pulled the hefty atlas down from his shelf. Together we pored over the geography of the island.

"It looks like a blue whale," I said.

"What?" He crinkled up his nose underneath the round glasses he always wore.

"The shape." I pointed.

"So it does," he said.

La Habana, Matanzas, Veradero, Cienfuegos, Trinidad, Santiago.... I read my way from west to east of the island, thinking: somewhere on this piece of paper my mother exists.

"Why are you so interested in Cuba?" the teacher asked.

"My mother's there."

"Gone on holiday, has she?"

"No, she's disappeared," I said.

"Well if you know she's in Cuba then she can't have disappeared," he reasoned.

"We don't know where she's gone," I explained. "But we think it might be Cuba."

"Oh," he said, and closed the atlas, closed the book on the face of my mother, staring up at me from between the inscrutable lines of highways and mountains and cities.

THE YEAR THAT SHE LEFT, my mother and I lived together in an apartment in an east-coast city whose sky was constantly lowering with the threat of rain. I liked the weather: the wind and the fierce wet seemed to agree with me, with the usual and sudden change of my moods that went from dull pessimism to outright despair. The rust-voiced cries of the seagulls pierced our day, and the foghorn groaned at precisely 1 a.m. every night, and I swore I would not go to sleep without hearing its unearthly sign. I told myself: That's what the dinosaurs would have sounded like, that's what the Loch Ness Monster sounds like when she comes up, furtively and always in the night, for air.

Our days were uniform. My mother went to her job at the university, wearing wraparound skirts and open toe sandals and make-up. I put on the dirty blue and grey anorak I wore every day, my old pair of floral-print jeans (refugees from some mid-seventies year) and put my greasy hair back in a ponytail. "MacPhail, MacPhail, she always had a greasy tail," the kids at school had always teased me. I wore nerdy clothes, I was a "brain," ergo: I was a nerd.

I sloshed to school the morning my mother introduced me to Lynne, much as any other morning. My unfashionable Zellers Adidas quickly got wet in the rain, and by the time I neared the Junior High I was squish-squishing along the sidewalk.

"Hi Anne," said Rita, my Indian friend. I say "Indian" because she was, first of all, and this seemed to mean something to some people, because she didn't have any other friends. Or maybe it's because she was very bright, and did not wear pink sweatsuits bought at Fairweather stores in shopping malls.

"What's the matter?" she asked.

"Nothing," I mumbled. "Got to get a drink," I said, and stopped by the water fountain.

When I bent down to the spout, I noticed my cheeks were wet, although it wasn't from the water. I drew back and bumped my head on the top of the fountain.

"What's the matter?" Rita asked again from behind me.

I couldn't speak. The bell for the first class saved me. I parted with my anorak and crossed the green-and-orange industrial airport coloured corridor, took a deep breath and opened the door to my class.

I AM FULLY OF THE FAITH that believes every daughter somehow turns into her mother. This is a religion of fear; I fear becoming my mother. Many women do; they in fact go steadfastly out of their ways to ensure that there is no chance that their own lives will be as mottled as their mother's bellies and thighs, that mistakes will not be miraculously repeated. But at the same time you believe that these things will come to pass, even though the conditions for their reappearance are adverse. Take my example: when my mother was twenty-two and a virgin, she got pregnant. Catholic and no husband. First of all, what kind of body is this we're locked into? What kind of insane asylum was I carting around with me every day, feeding and exercising? That you could get pregnant, bang! Never before, once, and then bang! Pregnant. One time, baby, and you're through.

"I threw up for months," my mother said.

My father, meanwhile, walked clean. Clean pants. No blood. Clean stomach, no streaks. Clean conscience. Cleaned out of me, dancing inside it.

My thin, androgynous, beautiful mother became pregnant. Her Catholicism alone should have prevented it. (But then I suspect she always wanted to do a reprise on the Virgin Birth.) She even went into a convent after I was born. Or was that before? If so, it didn't do her much good, did it?

And so I thought that I too would become pregnant at twenty-two, and that history would repeat itself in the most symmetrical and terrifying fashion. Never mind that I had never slept with a man, and had no intention of doing anything so ridiculous.

So I waited for divine intervention. I even took the pill, as a precautionary measure—as if that would confound the Gods. When I turned twenty-three, I breathed a sigh of profound relief. But I was still suspicious. There were so many mistakes you could make, as a woman. I wondered if men lived in an error-free world, and how so much less terrifying this would be. Meanwhile I knew some elliptical fate was waiting, revolving out there for me, cunning and simply biding its time until I relaxed my guard sufficiently to make the final mistake.

"DO YOU HAVE TO GO HOME?" my friends asked me when school let out. They were labouring under the stern stare of their mothers, who kept a sharp professional eye on them (mothers were invariably doctors or lawyers) and their fathers, who occasionally kept a sharp hand on them (fathers were invariably doctors or lawyers).

"No," I said. I never had to go home, but I went there anyway.

My mother came home sometimes after work, sometimes not.

In any case, I made my own supper and did my homework. I also did stained glass and Ukrainian Easter Eggs and various other hand-crafts. My mother would come home sometimes at 1 a.m. (just before the foghorn) smelling of smoke and wine, and would find me with my fingers in a pot of purple dye, hanging on to an egg in the advanced stages of decoration.

She never said: "Don't you think you ought to be in bed?" Or, "Wasting your time on an egg...shouldn't you be doing your homework?"

She never said motherly things at all. She just hung up her coat and went to bed. With my eyes, I followed her silk-clad back, until she entered the side room, the dark one, the one I used to share with her, and went to bed.

THE LETTER dropped down in front of me.

"What's this?" I was busy eating my granola.

"A letter from Grandma," she said.

"She's coming back?" I asked hopefully.

"Yes, it seems Aunt Ada and Aunt Vera are better."

I skipped to school that morning.

When Grandma had lived with us she had cooked breakfast for me every morning and supper every evening, even though she was very busy taking care of the Reichmanns, an elderly Jewish couple. She became quite fond of them, but even fonder of their cuisine.

"What's this?" I asked one evening.

"Matzo, try it. It's wonderful."

"It tastes like cardboard."

"It's unleavened bread. It's Passover now, so we shouldn't eat leavened bread," Grandma said solemnly and went to the pot to get some more Matzo balls.

"But we're Catholic," I protested.

"That doesn't matter," Grandma said. "And next there's gefilte fish."

Then she went home to the island, to care for Ada and Vera.

My mother and I were left looking at one another from across the table, her in her blue eye shadow and delicate faux-silk blouses, and me in my anorak.

"You're quite a tomboy," she said one evening when I came in from playing baseball outside. I was pleased because I had hit three home runs.

"What's that?"

"A girl who behaves like a boy."

"I'm a *girl?*"

"Don't be stupid."

"I'm not being stupid. So what if I'm a girl?"

"Oh well," she sighed, "you must be getting to That Age."

"What Age are you talking about? Am I going to die?"

She didn't answer, but went over to the round mirror in the hallway and checked her makeup. It was dark, and by the way the yellow streetlights outside had turned fuzzy and orange I could tell it had started to rain. The flat was quiet, and lonely, without Grandma.

"Are you going out?" I asked in a plaintive voice. I didn't want to be left alone that night.

"Yes, I'm off to the Newfoundland club." She said, "We'll be back after midnight sometime."

"Who's we?" I asked.

"Oh, I meant Grandma and I, but Grandma's not here anymore...." She looked away, into the mirror, where she saw something that seemed to be not entirely to her liking. She shrugged her shoulders and went to pick up her trenchcoat.

"Don't leave me alone," I pleaded. Even I knew I was being pathetic.

"I've got to go. It's arranged."

"Well, then take me sometimes...." I was beginning to whine.

"You're beginning to whine," she said sternly. "And it will be a good six years until you're allowed in a place like that."

And she was gone, into the night.

I HEARD THEM and thought: *sex.*

My mother's body, sacred to me, profane to her. About to be made base in my mind, as her body joined the TV and magazine pictures of it, the contorted and lurid images that flitted in my mind at night, their tuneless accompaniment and their graceless mocking of that word—sex.

What was it they did, that they had to exclude me so completely?

It sounded like pain. I think I would have chosen to howl in actual pain before I sounded like that. It sounded like abdication, the steady erasure of the soul. Mew, gasp, creak, gasp. A horrible cacophony of animals' witless throaty screams. I covered my ears and ran to my room. Gulping for breath once I got there, feeling my fingers tingle and tremble as a result of my hyperventilation. I got into bed and tried to smother myself with my pillow and comforter.

That will make her notice.

No luck. I was still breathing. I looked out the window, the grey northern night sky suffused with the pink blush of a thousand streetlights. What did she do for my mother that I could not? What was this wild animal that had invaded the house of our love and wrecked all the sturdiest furniture?

In the morning when she finds me dead she'll know why.

You must be able to will yourself to death, I considered. Most other things can, in some way, be willed, if one is strong enough. I began to put all my energy into an incantation inviting death. I saw the scenario (me, my skin sallow, purple bruises under my eyes that the undertaker would try to cover up, muttering "so young, so young, it's her mother's fault, you know...." My lips still with a maddening cherry red in them, as if still alive). I heard the mantra-like music, a deep basso profundo, willing me on through thick woods smothered by snow. It looked like winter, death. That seemed right. I was travelling toward it, thinking.

I hope she dies of guilt.

I fell asleep. When I woke up in the morning I was still alive.

I KNEW LYNNE BY SMELL. She wore perfume, and not a mass-produced department store scent; she wore something quite extraordinary, which smelled of bluebells and cherry blossoms and wet green earth. Although she was French—from France, not Quebec—she smelled like England, or what I imagined England to smell like, after reading many nostalgia-infused English novels like *Brideshead Revisited* and *Howard's End*.

The first time I met her she and my mother were smoking, which was strange, because my mother didn't smoke. There is something quite obscene about watching a non-smoker raise a cigarette to her mouth. She looked wrong, like a bad actress assuming a part she knows is not for her.

"You don't smoke," I said.

"Is that any way to say hello to someone?" She looked at Lynne. "She's forgotten her manners."

"That's not true. I don't have any manners," I said.

Lynne looked at me—coolly, I think is the word. That appraising glance that women have, which takes you in from head to toe in one flickering movement from the eyes and which forms judgements as fast as it forms visual impressions. She continued to smoke.

"I wish you wouldn't smoke. It kills people. In forty years I'll be dead and I'll have never smoked a cigarette once in my life."

My mother's eyes narrowed.

"Hello," Lynne said. She dropped her "h" slightly. "I'm Lynne. You must be Anne. Your mother has told me much about you."

"Well my mother hasn't told me a thing about you, but that's not unusual," I said, and left to go to my room.

I could hear them murmuring in my wake. I liked unsettling people. I wanted to give Lynne a taste of what she was in for if she wanted to "make friends." Adults, or at least friends of my mother's, seemed to regard me as some sort of emotional poker chip, or a bargaining clause in a daunting industrial dispute. I didn't understand why, as my mother seemed to pay little attention to me. But all the same I knew that I was being used.

Men did not come by frequently. There were two Jonathans with whom she was friends. I got them mixed up, as they looked alike. These Jonathans were my rivals, sure enough, just as this woman Lynne was. I don't know why, but from the beginning I recognized immediately—with that terrifying emotional X-ray vision prepubescents can have—the nature of their relationship. I saw her in the same way I regarded the men who came to call on my mother at home.

I didn't understand the mechanics of sex, or what indeed the sexual relationship was built upon. It just seemed to me that with these people—the two Jonathans and Lynne—what my mother had stepped into was some kind of quagmire, some place where the ground shifted constantly; where nothing was certain and where cruelty was just around the next corner. And she had taken me there with her, whether I liked it or not, because I loved her.

LYNNE: A NARROW FACE, a stark chin. Dark brown eyes, a small but slightly crudely-shaped nose. Dark hair pulled back like a ballerina. She moves like a dancer, in fact, and always wears long flowing dresses that are belted or otherwise brought in at the waist. Her torso and waist are hard, her back straight. She is muscled, but that muscularity is feline, as it often is with women. I do not like this. It signals danger, transgression, cunning. But I can see very well, without even thinking about it, that she is beautiful. Not as beautiful as my mother, but she has grace.

They have long, tortured conversations with one another on the phone. They speak half in English, half in French. They imagine I can't, with my grade-school French, understand what they are saying to one another, but secretly I am reading Balzac, so I understand their language of exhortations and florid entreaties (all uttered in the sensual monotone of the language) very well. Once or twice I listen in on their phone conversations, but their sentiments are torrid, embarrassing, and my ears turn red. I put the phone down gently. I know I am a "mole": the spy within. I know I could make my mother cry by telling her that I listen in to her nightly conversations on the other extension. One day soon I will.

THE NEXT DAY I bump into her and Lynne on the sidewalk downtown. I knew they would be there, because I heard them arrange their meeting outside the Public Gardens on Spring Garden Road on the telephone the night before. But I have not tried to bump into them. I am just going about my business, coming back from the library. I see them ahead of me, on the wide sidewalk outside the Public Gardens. My mother wears her grey trenchcoat, businesslike and professional. Lynne wears a corduroy jacket and a flowered skirt. Next to my mother she looks small, like a moon orbiting a planet.

As I approach them I realize they have seen me, and there is no escape. I have to walk past them. The street is too wide to cross, the gardens cordoned off by a tall cast-iron fence. As I come upon them I see their faces, blank, expectant, waiting for the inevitable confrontation. Lynne's thin French lips are set, pursed. My mother's face is expressionless. I keep my face down once I have charted the coordinates of their position. I brush by them, even as they look incredulously at me. I jostle Lynne as I walk by, saying nothing, walking straight ahead.

I know this moment contains a crime, and that I will never be able to rescind either the action or the moment, that this moment will go on echoing down the corridors of my life, and their lives, for years to come. That its ghost will always loiter near me.

When I get home I put the two tins of consommé soup, which my mother asked me to get at the supermarket, on the table. I go to my room to wait for the echoes of my decision to reach my ears.

I LOVED MY MOTHER SO MUCH I thought I would die of it, the putrid jealousy I felt when she seemed ready to place her love and allegiance elsewhere, with someone else. I loved her so that she could only have been a traitor, she could only have betrayed me. Because to return my love at its own pitch, on its own frequency, would have been to become my lover, in a way. I was that needy of her, of the idea of her, of the scent of her past and her secretive nature, her undisclosed experiences.

I wanted it to be her and me only in the universe, forever.

We would have been together. There would have been no one left but us, and no one would have been able to penetrate our conspiracy of those who remember the same experiences, who would be alone in those memories if not for the other.

These were the old, saltwater ropes that bound us together, like the ropes securing the abandoned ferry at the waterfront to its dock; they were twisted with kelp like Christmas decorations. They creaked and stretched with every heave of the tide.

Our love. The landscape of our hearts; similar, known.

Until she left me there alone, on the flat marshy fields, a landscape without contour or relief or a high point from which to form a perspective. Alone, without the person whose boundaries somehow crossed with mine and merged us, without our even understanding it, into one.

"I'M NOT YOUR LOVER." My mother's voice was hard. It was the most brutal and the most tender thing she had ever said.

"But you're everything to me," I said.

"I'm not your lover," she repeated.

I was shocked. So shocked that I forgot to launch my final, desperate salvo.

"I belong with you."

"You belong with yourself," is what she would have said.

HEAVY STEPS sounded on the staircase.

"It's Grandma!" I yelled, and ran to the door. And it was. There she was, sweating and breathing heavily. She stood in the doorway and wiped her glasses, then she looked at me with her lips pursed. I stopped smiling. Pursed lips meant Grandma was very mad.

"Your mother..." she began, and then ran out of breath. "Fiona was supposed to pick me up from the bus station," she breathed. "I was on that bus for five hours and then I waited in the bus station for another hour."

"Why didn't you just get a cab?"

"How the Jesus do you think I got here? Now get my bags."

"I think my mother's out with her friend," I said to Grandma later as I sunk the three tea bags into the kettle. "That's why she forgot to pick you up."

Grandma sat heavily down into the chair at the kitchen table and began to rub her feet. "You're not making that damn dishwater tea again are you?" she barked. "And who is this friend?"

"Um...Lynne is her name."

"Oh...," Grandma mumbled. "I thought it might have been...."

"What?" I turned around.

"Don't you what me," she retorted.

"But you're always after me not to mumble," I complained.

"Respect your betters and your elders," she quipped.

Grandma was back.

MY MOTHER WAS BEAUTIFUL. Even I was aware of that, walking down the street or in the shopping mall with her. People looked at her; never at me. I began to feel like a downtrodden servant following her elegant mistress around, walking with my arms splayed open like a human trolley, waiting for posh packages to be stacked on top. But in any case everyone looked at her. Didn't she mind? I wondered. I hated it when people looked at me. But they looked at her in a very different way.

My mother's face was very delicate. A long, straight nose. Pale blue eyes, a thinnish but well-formed mouth, and delicate but strong cheekbones. She had the inoffensively perfect face of a china doll when pale, or of an adventuress when tanned. She was everything and anything she wanted to be, because she was beautiful. That seemed to be her destiny—I was beginning to understand it was the favoured destiny of women, to be beautiful.

And then there was her mystery (this was probably also related to beauty). It seemed to be one of the keys to the room in which great strapping pieces of furniture were piled: mahogany escritoires, teak wardrobes, various stocky commodes. This was the furniture of her heart. They were heavy, yet she carried these things everywhere with her. In their locked drawers were the secrets to her soul; and on those faded pieces of parchment were written, in code, the reasons why I would never know her.

"I HEARD YOU COMING HOME pretty late last night, Fiona." My grandmother shot her a poisonous look.

"Mmn," my mother said.

"And I heard another woman's voice," Grandma said. "Is that one of the girlfriends you go out carousing with? You've got your job to think of, don't you think?"

"My job is not my life and I do it very well nonetheless thank you."

My mother could retreat from what she perceived as any invasion of her privacy with an icy resolve that made re-launching any attempt to break it quite futile. She even managed to perform this on my grandmother.

"I have to go back to bed," I said, and went to my room.

I could hear their muffled arguing.

"...Now I know we like to have our fun but why do you have to go out all the time and not take me anymore?" (Grandma.)

"...don't go to the Newfoundland club...." (My mother.)

"Then where.... What the devil are you doing...?" (Grandma.)

I thought I heard the slamming of doors but I was losing the struggle to stay awake. I slept heavily, a sleep invaded by terrible dreams. I saw white-faced women intertwined like snakes, writhing, dancing, naked women running, screaming, through the hallways, my mother laughing, riding hippopotamuses....

"Anne!"

"What?" I struggled to free myself from the tentacles of sleep.

It was my grandmother, burst into my room like a character from a bad television show. She was breathing heavily. Her glasses were steamed up.

"Your mother's gone!"

It was all she could say, before she collapsed like a heap of old washing.

MY MOTHER DISAPPEARED.

"You're not to speak of your mother," said my grandmother, in between visits from the RCMP, who were looking for my mother. They had located an airline which had given them her name. That's what they came to tell my grandmother on their last visit to us.

We had no more money to stay in the apartment in the city. We had to move to a housing block where most people were on welfare or Valium, or both. The doctor prescribed Valium for my grandmother too, and soon she had a glassy-eyed look about her and she couldn't remember what day it was or whether we had any milk in the house.

"DO YOU REALIZE you've stopped menstruating?"

I looked at the doctor as if to say, What? You think that's a bad thing? But I couldn't say anything the whole time he questioned me.

The doctor called my grandmother in and said: "She's very depressed. I would recommend anti-depressants, Valium and force-feeding."

At that I perked up. "I'm fine," I said. "Just fine. Where's the yoghurt?"

"Anne." My grandmother looked at me sternly. "This is not a game."

"He's not going to put me on Valium," I swore. "I'm not going to end up like a zombie like you just because my mother ran off to Cuba with another woman."

The doctor looked at me. "What's this about her mother?" he finally asked my grandmother.

"None of your business," my grandmother snapped, glaring at me.

On the bus on the way home my grandmother shoved me up against the window. "You're going to have to smarten up and start eating. There's no use mooning over your mother. I got a postcard from her, you know. I was going to tell you but I wanted to wait until you were better. It says she's coming back in a few months."

"She's coming back?" I nearly jumped out of my seat. And then the timescale hit me. "A few months?" I slumped down again. "That's forever."

"Never you mind," said my grandmother. "Now let's go to the Mall." We jumped off the bus and got on the one for the Shopping Centre. We were wandering around the makeup section of Eaton's, fingering the tiny cases of blue eye shadow. *My mother wears this*, I thought. *She puts it on in neat half-moon circles above her eyes.* I wondered if that's what she was doing, right then, in Cuba.

"Will I turn into a lesbian?"

"Shhh." Grandma hauled me away into the scarf section and looked around like a fugitive. "Who taught you that word?"

"I looked it up in the dictionary. That's what Mummy is."

"She is not. She's perfectly normal." My grandmother released my sleeve and I tumbled into a bin of $10.99 brightly-coloured silk scarves.

"Come on, I'll buy you an ice cream."

When we were sitting down on one of the yellow plastic benches and I was licking my first raspberry ripple ice cream in months, Grandma took my hand.

"I want you to mark my words, you hear?" This is what she always said when she had something important to tell me.

"Your mother went away because I wasn't very nice to her. Do you know that?"

I shook my head.

"I told her she was the devil incarnate and that she was queer."

I stopped licking my ice cream. It began to drip down my fingers.

"Now I was wrong." My grandmother's lips were set in a thin line. "And she was right to go away. But I don't want you thinking that it was your fault or that you had anything to do with it. I wrote to Fiona and told her that I would love her no matter what she was or who she loved and that I wouldn't judge her. And I'll tell you the same thing."

"Now don't cry." She whipped a Kleenex out of her purse. "I'll take care of you no matter what happens. "

FOUR MONTHS LATER my mother came back. Lynne returned to France, and my mother returned to her job. She was very tanned. She and my grandmother went out to the Newfoundland club together. I did my geography project that term on Cuba, and my sociology project on lesbianism. My classmates began to think I was a bit strange. But this didn't bother me. I had my mother back. She was just as beautiful as she had always been, I was going on to Junior High School in the fall, and now it was a warm spring. The crocuses were out and the buds were ripening on the trees. My mother and I wandered together in Point Pleasant Park and ate ice cream. She told me about Cuba: about the fabulous beaches and the sugarcane-cutting collectives and the poor people who nonetheless had their own homes and televisions.

"It's a kind of low-level paradise," she laughed.

I didn't quite understand so I told her about the homosexuals in Fidel Castro's prisons, which I had learned when I was researching both my Cuba and my lesbianism projects. My mother looked sad, and I began to wish I hadn't told her.

"Why are you sad?" I said.

"Because such terrible things can happen in such beautiful places."

I nodded. I didn't really understand what she meant. The character of her sadness was entirely adult. She seemed to know something she had to forget, like most adults do. I wasn't sure I wanted to understand her, but I knew that she was back and we would be together. Not in the way I had once wanted, that was true. But we would be together.

The Day the Men Went to Town

TESSIE GILLIS

WINTER WAS ANGRY even by Island standards. Ever since the first flurry of snowflakes in November, the winds had been busy shifting the drifts into strange shapes and forms, but it wasn't until after Christmas that winter really began. I hardly took the time to tie my shoes in the morning before rushing to the window to see what new pictures the night winds had drawn.

It was barely dawn and already Jim had shovelled his way out of the house, cut a path to the barn, the chicken house, the toilet and to the spring. In places the drifts had been higher than a man's head.

Jim sat now, taking long draughts of tea and staring at the list of groceries I had left on the table.

"Best get your pencil and start cutting," he said. There was no trace of resentment in his voice. "The Beatons and Lauchie must be out o' groceries, and your list will fill a whole sleigh."

"I can't cut much," I said, picking up the pencil. "We'll have to have flour—a hundred pounds, then with the potatoes and vegetables I canned we won't go hungry—as long as the meat holds out...we're out of baking powder...I can cut the rolled oats...lard? I suppose I could render some of the fat off the salt pork...matches...both kinds of soap...the dry beans can be halved, macaroni too. Ten pounds of sugar won't last for long, but I suppose it will have to do...salt...I can't cut any more. Heaven alone knows when you'll get out again. I'd better put tobacco and the papers down too, or you'll forget them." I

91

pencilled in "one bag of candy," Jim could put that in his pocket. Jim never forgot to bring candy for the children, still it wouldn't do any harm to remind him.

"Bells!" said Jim jumping up from the table. "They're coming. On this of all days they have to come early. Must've started at midnight."

"Why are you in such a dither? Don't they always come early?"

"Yeh! But I ain't got that end of the road open yet."

"So what! They're early, you're late. There's no harm done."

"That ain't the point! I DIDN'T GET THE ROAD OPEN YESTERDAY!"

Jim's face was flushed with anger. "Time I got through with that whore of a shovel it was milking time."

"But there was a storm—you had a good excuse. They didn't come down on account of the storm."

"Cut it out, Mary, will ye!"

Yesterday had been a bad day. The blizzard had lasted for nearly two days. The temperature had fallen to five below zero. Jim had managed to cut a path to the spring to water the animals when the trouble started. The first bit of the shovel went deep into four feet of snow that covered the spring, but when he tried to pull it out heaped with snow, the handle broke just where it joined the spoon. Frost had made the wood brittle. By the time he had taken the stub out, taped the handle and set it back in the spoon, it had been time to feed the animals and clean the stables. It was too late to start opening the road. Jim had been ferocious. His hands had been stiff with cold, his frozen mitts had stuck to the metal shovel.

"Jim! Look! Harold's mare is in a drift," I shouted from the window. "They're all around him."

"Jesus! Jesus!" said Jim, fumbling with his jacket. "The only day in a month I missed opening the road, they have to come early. I'll be the shit of the Glen after this."

"Cut it out, Jim. A person would think the world was coming to an end all because you didn't open the road. Tell them about Silver.

92

They'll not think it's your fault...."

"NO! They'll know damn well it IS my fault. Where's me mitts? It would have to be on MY stretch of road. Hurry! 'Fore they'll be telling everyone I sat in the house and wouldn't give them a hand!"

It was only last week that Silver had buried herself in a drift. I had never seen a frightened animal before. I watched the little mare writhe, her body covered with foam. I saw the spasms that shook her withers and her eyes full of tears. We took Silver home and led her into her stall. Billows of steam rose from her body; her eyes rolled with hysterics as Jim tenderly rubbed her down. I stood beside her talking gently into her ear as I stroked her foaming neck. It seemed hours before the drops of saliva stopped flowing—drops that turned to ice pellets before reaching the ground. Then we covered her with a blanket and bedded her down. Ever since that day I knew Jim would be reluctant to take Silver out after a storm.

Jim was running down the yard. Harold had calmed the mare with his petting. Jim started shovelling like a madman. In a few minutes the mare was free, and the little procession turned up the short road into the yard. Harold Beaton came first leading his pigeon-toed Queenie, straining at the huge stump hooked to the "swing" that packed the snow down hard and cleared a wider path than a log would have done. Queenie was the best snow horse on the Settlement Road because she was wise enough to stop and wait for Harold to shovel her out when the snow was too deep. Close behind her came Jennie, Joe Beaton's much-loved mare. Small, black, sway-backed, she drew a long log wrapped in logging chains. Last of all came Lauchie's big grey mare. Head up, nostrils flaring, proud and haughty, as though she pulled the fanciest of carriages instead of a homemade wood sleigh. "Them wood-sleds! Coldest things on earth. I'd be warmer walkin' in me shirt sleeves than bundled up riding on one o' them," Jim always said.

The men would be looking for tea! I prodded and turned the damp sticks in the range, trying to coax them to burn. I put out the cups and saucers and cut the bread. They were putting Jennie in the stable. Lauchie and Harold Beaton took their horses to the fence, tied and blanketed them there. "They must be taking two sleighs today," I said to myself.

The men pushed open the door and lumbered over to the stove. They took off their mitts and stood rubbing their hands in what little warmth they could find. There was little to distinguish the three men. Their long-billed caps with the fur-lined ear flaps hung over the collars of their jackets and their heavy woolen trousers ballooned out over their tightly laced boots like sausages.

"Devil take this place," said Jim as he closed the door behind him. "No phone, no lights, no plow, no nothin'.... Nova Scotia, the place God forgot!" Jim clasped his lips together as if he dared anyone to defy him.

"That's not true, Jim! The place God REMEMBERS is more like it. Next winter we'll have the plow. I've written to the Minister and to the engineer, and we'll have electric light and a telephone too, you'll see."

"That'll be the day!" said Jim, throwing off his coat.

"Breaking roads, now that all them farms is empty," said Lauchie, trying to cover up for my breach of good manners in "answering back" my husband. "Takes all a man's time in winter."

"They have to be opened," said Harold. "A single track any-way's, else it's 'good-bye.'"

"Going to town is an all-day job, all right," added Joe Beaton, taking his place at the table. "Even when there is a track." The men ate and drank in silence.

"Thank ye for the tea, Mary," said Lauchie, pushing back his chair and crossing over to the back door where their dripping jackets hung on a row of nails. He turned to Joe Beaton. "Ye be after going on my sleigh, Joe?"

"Me? Naw, I'll wait down at Dougall's. Harold'll be needin' a hand when he gets back. Thought I'd wait there."

Jim stopped and turned to me as he buttoned up his coat. "I don't know when we'll be back. Never mind the stables." Then he followed the men out and closed the door behind him. Jim knew, and I knew, that the stables would be cleaned before he returned.

I HOPE THERE WON'T BE ANY CALLERS. I have so much work to do and the day will be gone so quickly. The sun is a stranger most days now and it is a shame to miss a good day's drying. Will I ever be able to get the big wash and Sonny's diapers done as well? Not with all the outside chores...still I must try. It is a blessing that Joe Beaton is going to spend the day at Dougall's and not here, in my kitchen like he usually does. I hate washing diapers in front of a bachelor. How many times have I had to gather everything up in a rush and hide them in the pantry—any place to get them out of sight, when one of the Beatons or MacTavishes calls unexpectedly.

How shocked my sisters would be if they could see me now! A pile of dirty diapers on the floor—and they aren't all diapers either; many are pieces of worn-out undergarments salvaged from the ragbag. My crooked old washtub standing on two chairs facing each other, seats touching. The family chamber pot in the centre of the room ready for the diapers after their first rough wash.

I put the washboard in the tub, then half fill a smaller tub with cold water, carry it over to the stove and pour in boiling water from the kettle. I balance it carefully on the edge of the stove and test the water with the other hand. It is just hot enough. Then I put it down beside the chamber pot and I kneel down. The little ones are playing quietly now in the other room, thank God! I wonder if Lauchie and the Beatons will stay the night? It will depend on how early they get back. If they stay, there will be four for cards and I won't have to play. I don't care much for playing cards, I'd rather watch, and when the time comes for tea I won't have to jump up between dealings to get things ready, or to keep the fire going. It's nice having company though. I get tired listening to the radio every night...the batteries are nearly gone, too...I'll have to order new ones on the budget plan...the bill at the store is too high to add any luxuries...if the weather doesn't break soon so that Jim can get into the woods for pit timber the store might stop our credit...but if the weather changes we'll be all right. God is good! How pretty Anne looked in her pink blouse...I was right...the colour brought out the pink in her complexion. "Pink wouldn't look right with her red hair," Clemmie said. But what does she know? Anne has the roundest, the bluest eyes I've ever seen...they dance with mischief and make you want to be a part of her fun—her laughter...Anne loves everything and everyone...and Sonny is so smart! Talking already...walking and running everywhere...no single steps for him...no single words either...from the very first it had been sentences...he is wise beyond his years, and it shows in his grey eyes...his little face must be startling to strangers...Sonny is so different from other children.

I get up and stretch, to relieve the strain from crouching on the floor for so long. I'll have to dry some of the diapers on the line over the stove. I pick up the little tub of brown smelly water and carry it over to the door. I don't bother to put on my coat. It will only take a few seconds to throw the water out into the snow. That done, I pick up the big kettle of boiling water and stagger over to the tub. I pour the water, slowly at first, so as not to splatter and scald myself. I don't really mind washing, it gives me a kind of buoyance. I can feel the rhythm of the rubbing on the washboard...and my hands bobbing in and out of the water—it feels like part of a dance. The slapping together of the wet clothes, the swirling movement of the water, and the splatter of large drops when I lift a garment to cool, sounds like rain on a stagnant pool. I wish my back wouldn't ache so, and why should streaks of pain dart into my shoulders? No suds! And after using a whole bar of soap! The water is silent and dead; even with a tub of hot water I can't get a single bubble, the water is so hard.

I watch the last drop fall from the diaper; I twist it and stack it on the chair like cord wood. I swish my hand round in the water. There is nothing left to wash; my hand catches the side of the tub. That place is dangerous. Tubs don't last long around here. There are too many uses for them—Saturday night's baths, the washing and butchering. Jim had used this one to catch the entrails of a steer he butchered for Christmas. That is when it got bent. It will have to last until spring.

I don't know when the silence started. All at once everything is stifled, smothered, as if there had been a fall of goosefeathers so thick that I can't breathe. Silence in a house with children? That means mischief. I had learned that long ago. I kick off my slippers and tiptoe to the door and peer in. There they are, the two of them, sitting on the floor close to the back wall; sitting in a circle of pieces of wallpaper—Anne's little hand grasping a frayed end still clinging to the wall and gently ripping it off the plaster board. I wanted to burst out laughing. Spanking them is hard but I have to do it or we won't have any paper left on the walls. I didn't really hurt them and they soon forget all about it and go on playing with their toys.

It had been fun to wash at home in Montana where clothes came out of the water gleaming white, but how can I get clothes white when the water is brackish and there isn't enough of it? Jim warned me to go easy because the water hole is going dry. He doesn't think there will be enough for the cows for another week, and Clemmie told me that she remembers when the people who used to live here had to take the cows down to the spring near the river in cold weather—and that is a whole mile away. The snow had to be cleared away before the cattle could reach the water and then someone had to stand by until they had finished drinking. Sometimes if a heavy frost followed a thaw, the cows couldn't cross the ice to get near enough to the spring to drink.

THANK HEAVENS! Only the rinsing to be done. I stretch my back again. What was that? A racket in the barn? It's noon already. No wonder the cows are complaining. All animals make a fuss when they are thirsty. I had better take a look. They'll have to wait for their hay until I feed the children and settle them down for their nap.

I put on my coat and rubbers and run down the yard. I throw open the door to the cow stable and brace it to the wall with a big stick, and step inside. It isn't until my eyes have grown accustomed to the half-darkness that I can see the burning eyes not two feet away. The bull! He must have broken out of his stall. And there he is standing behind the cows with a length of frayed rope round his neck. I can feel a constriction in my throat. My mouth is dry. I can't speak. I can't move. My senses come back slowly. I feel the pounding of my heart. Slowly I step back into the open doorway and quickly kick the prop aside and slam the door. What am I to do? I can't leave him there. Most of the cows are heavy with calf; they are wrenching at their chains, trying to free themselves. What can I do? I must try to get him back into his own stall beside Silver and across the threshing floor. I'll have to get behind him. But how? The only way is to crawl through one of the cows' feeding bins. Making sure that the door is secure, I run over to the "little people's door" cut in the big double doors that are only opened for the haymaking. The bull hears me and turns. Then he stands still and glares at me for a moment before pawing the gutter. Oh, God! Joe Beaton has stabled Jennie in the stall beyond Silver's, and if the bull passes his own stall and Silver's and reaches the mare, he'll gore her or she'll kick at him. Jennie'll kick at anything. She even kicks the boards of her own stall for want of something to do. I'll have to build a barricade of some kind to stop the bull passing his own stall, that is, if I can get him back that way at all.

There's a pile of old boards that Jim has left stacked in the corner. I pull out board after board. Thank goodness! Some of them are long enough to stretch from the wall to the end of the stall. But how am I going to support the boards? There is nothing but an old puncheon. I push and haul the puncheon over and use it as a brace. I slant some of the boards so that they slide in between the rails of the bull's stall. Perhaps the puncheon will keep them in position. It's heavy enough. Jennie is getting restive now, pulling at her halter and stamping her feet. Then she kicks with both of her hind legs. The beating of hooves against the walls of her stall sounds like thunder, but my barricade holds in spite of the shaking posts that anchor them. Now I'll have to reach the far side of the bull. How can I manage that? I could go outside and climb in through the little dung window...crawl through on my belly and then drop to the floor. No! I couldn't do that! There's another way. I can crawl through into a feeding bin in front of one of the cows, slide past her to reach the gutter. I walk down the length of the barn, passing each cow. Which stall shall I try? Star's? Poor gentle Star. Jim says she's so gentle that "she'd feel terrible if she even bumped ye!"

I open the clapper and look in. There's Star, but her eyes are now fiery and her nose so huge that a piece of paper couldn't be squeezed past. Perhaps I can get past one of the calves. Their horns are shorter. I run down to the other end of the barn. A pitchfork would be useful! I had better take it along. I can use it to drive the bull—if I ever reach him. I open a clapper to the calves' stall. Calves these animals might be, but they are spring calves, half grown, and now they look as big as elephants. I drop the clapper and look at my watch. The men have only been gone a few hours, and it might be seven or eight o'clock before they get back. I lift the clapper again. "Talk! Talk! Talk!" I say to myself. It will keep your teeth from chattering...take a deep breath...stand still until you stop shaking. Now! Open the clapper, stick the fork through first...leave the handle sticking out so that it will hold the lid up a little...now, first one leg...that's it...up and over...now bend down and put your head in. Quick! Squeeze your body through...hold your breath...there isn't much room but the calf's as far over as he can get...he looks frightened...he's in shock...but watch him...watch him. Why didn't I put the button on the clapper to hold it up...too late now...MOVE...keep going...look out! The calf! He's coming out of shock...quick...grab the fork...hold it before his eyes...go on...go on...the other foot...keep looking at the calf...he's getting bolder...he's getting MAD! Hurry! Hurry! Your feet are dangling...what's caught? Oh, Lord! His eyes are rolling now...I can't move...it must be my coat...take your mitts off...they're too thick, darned too much...I can't feel anything...the calf is edging nearer...Oh, God! If only this awful noise would stop...my hands will have to work...all those cows bellowing like cattle driven to the stockyards back home...that's got it! I'm free!

Oh...the fork is stuck in a board...my weight must have driven it in...it's jammed...the calf is coming nearer....

I can't remember how I pulled the fork free and got through the stall. My memory didn't start working again until I found myself in the gutter with the bull. As soon as I passed him the calf started a wild twisting tantrum, pulling at his halter and roaring. Another second and he would have killed me. Now Daisy is frisking! I should have remembered that Daisy was due. It was she who brought the bull over. If only I had remembered I could have left the door opened, untied Daisy and driven the two of them out into the yard. They wouldn't have bothered anyone. It's too late now, I can never crawl back past that calf.

Holding the fork before me I inch my way along the gutter behind the twisting bellowing cows. The bull turns his head and looks at me. I jab the fork straight at his rump. He jumps and turns to face me. I jab again, this time at the neck, but in order to get a straight jab, I have to back into Daisy's stall because of the length of the fork handle. Daisy is incensed and lashes out with her hind leg. I feel pain tear through my knee...again I strike the bull. Slowly and very independently he turns and moves forward in the direction of his stall. Once he starts, he keeps going until he reaches the treadway at the end of the barn and without prompting turns onto the threshing floor. I follow close behind, jabbing him every now and then to keep him moving.

Reaching the centre of the threshing floor, he becomes aware of the space around him, or perhaps because he doesn't like being pushed around, he turns suddenly and faces me. Fortunately the manure shovel stands within my reach. I grab it with my left hand and by holding it near the heavy end I find I can manage the fork in one hand and the shovel in the other. Still jabbing with the fork I raise the shovel before the bull's eyes...he moves forward...I side-step...he moves forward...I jab again...I don't want to give him time to think or brace himself for a charge. At last I have him facing in the direction of his own stall.

Then without warning he lets out a wild roar that shakes the barn to its foundations. He lowers his head and begins dragging his hoof slowly across the ground. With a crack like a pistol shot he strikes his own belly. I watch him helplessly. Without thinking I drop the fork, scoop up a pile of hayseed from the floor and throw it into his eyes. Then I pick up the fork and run across to a short ladder that leads up into the hay loft. The bull is quiet now. He shakes his head and blinks his eyes. I pull off my coat and drive the fork through the collar again and again, pleating the cloth to prevent it from slipping off the prongs. Then I lower it and the coat, fluttering like a pirate's flag in front of the bull at the entrance to his stall. For a moment he looks at the fluttering coat with indifference, then, as if he had just found his enemy, he lowers his head and charges. As I had hoped, the momentum of his charge carries him into his own stall. I drop the fork, scramble down the ladder and grasp the shafts of the hay rake that stands at the head of the threshing floor. I pull the unwieldy machine across the entrance to the stall. The cows are safe!

I kneel down and crawl underneath the hayrake to retrieve my coat. I am shivering now, and exhausted. I lie there for a minute to rest, until my breathing becomes more regular. I soon find the machine over me oppressive, and besides, my nostrils are full of dust. I crawl out, brush the hay from my clothes and put on my coat, then I close the barn door behind me and walk up the yard towards the house. The children are still playing quietly, they haven't even noticed that I had left the house. Thank God, I only have the rinsing left to do.

The Finger

TRICIA FISH

*T*HIS RELATIONSHIP would set the precedent for the rest of my life.

There was a phase during Grade Five with just Callum and I, where I would just hang around and watch him do stuff. I would go to Callum's house, a clean and groomed white house with green trim, and knock on the back door, and his mother would answer, and smile and nod, and call to Callum as if he were an adult. Mrs. Donahue was so dignified, intelligent, polite, and kind; these qualities terrified me into whispering. I wanted a mother like that sometimes, although I wouldn't really trade for anything. Everyone knew my mother was the best.

Anyway, Mrs. Donahue had short shiny dark hair with waves, not dyed, just quality hair. I remember sitting at the kitchen table, waiting for Callum, feeling like my limbs would knock something over if I moved. The phone rang and she answered it in a manner unfamiliar to me at the time. "Hello" had three syllables. He-lo-o? With a tolerant question mark at the end. I always felt transparent in their neat, tasteful house with the desk lamp on the kitchen table near the window to make it easier to do homework. I obsessed about how hideously skinny my legs were, and how huge my feet were. I was tall. I had growing pains in my stomach sometimes. My hair was greasy and in my eyes. I look back at photographs and feel angry my mother didn't make me wash my hair more often or make me cut my bangs. My mother was liberal. My father probably wanted me to be reined in, and Mum didn't care; if she thought it was the fashion, she'd indulge me. I was always telling her what the fashion was, or she watched me for it, or something. I mean, it's only bangs, but we have these huge rationalizations. So that we don't have to think at that point she just didn't give a shit.

Anyway, once outside, Callum dribbled a basketball in the paved backyard, near where the dogs were in a fenced kennel. They were yellow labs, strangers. I would lean against the back porch, trying to be shorter than I was, because Callum was shorter and we all know that's no good if I want to seem like the Girl of His Dreams. And he'd basically ignore me as he tried to shoot hoops. I mean, to think of it now, it was something we sort of agreed to do. It wasn't playing, and it wasn't talking, but it was related. There were no long conversations about anything. We had all verbal exchanges in short, terse, neatly written notes, folded and passed in class. In reality, there was silence.

Some days were special. They were when no one was home. He would lead me inside, through the empty house, up the stairs behind the piano, and once on the landing to the left, to his room. His room was really nice, with plaid bedspreads, and wood, and clean because obviously his mother cleaned his room for him. (There were two types of mothers: those who cleaned your room, and those who didn't. Mine did not. My room was insanely chaotic. But I couldn't allow my mother to wade in there and start to organize things. She was essentially disorganized, anyway. The cereal was tucked next to the pots, the peanut butter next to the mugs, etc. I had my own system. I had my papers, books, drawings, love notes, diary, magazines, my clothes—dirty and clean—everything, piled around the bed like a moat. Books were spread in a lumpen spray on the bedspread. No one could touch it.)

In Callum's room, on the second floor overlooking the driveway, I sat quietly while he tied flies. Fly-fishing flies. He was good at it. They were neat, balanced, pretty. Once he gave me one, and I wasn't sure what it meant.

Anyway, he tied flies...but I thought we were there for a reason that he was just getting geared up to reveal. A defining reason. I wanted to kiss. I was just watching his hands, saying nothing. Didn't he get it? Watching him clip a black thread.... Silence. I was confused. I still know those hands so well, from the hours watching them tie flies. This happened many, many times. Finally, Callum's lovely smooth tanned hands would finish, he would stand, and lead me back downstairs—without touching my hand—and I would walk home, alone.

But this day, after watching him for hours, him with his back to me, as I sat on the neat bed, feeling the rough texture of the bedspread against my bare legs, watching his head bowed a little over a little clamp, winding string around and around, tying it, clipping it, choosing a red thread, winding that around and around, I felt desperate that something should happen.... I finally stood up. He didn't say anything. I headed for the door, instead of waiting for him to finish and lead me downstairs again. I stared at him and sighed. He still said nothing. So I walked down the stairs and through the kitchen and out the door. This was it. I had snapped. No more. Outside, on the driveway, I looked up at his window; my heart was broken. Then his face appeared.

I waited for a wave, or for him to open the window and call me back. I waited for anything. But he was unbreakable. Placid. Emotionless. Nothing. Before I knew what I was doing, and for the first time in my life, I lifted my fist and stuck my middle finger in the air. I gave him the finger.

He just watched me. No reaction. I turned and walked quickly away, burst into tears, and sobbed as I walked from his street to mine on the next block. I was so painfully ashamed of myself. That nice house. His nice mother. He was so quiet. It was very confusing. He didn't do anything bad to me, why was I being so crazy?

This relationship would set the precedent for the rest of my life.

Passage by Water

JOAN CLARK

EMILY DIDN'T SEE THE FACE of the night nurse though the same woman came into her hospital room three nights in a row and shone a flashlight at her. The round blinding arc swept through the dark, across the metal bed, a searchlight tracking a lone prisoner in a night compound.

The first time the night nurse came into her room Emily was hallucinating. Ten days before she'd had her bladder repaired, a necessity after childbearing. Before the operation it had flopped down loosely, shapeless as a collapsed balloon, which meant she spilled urine whenever she jumped, ran or sneezed. Now her bladder was sewn to her pubic bone, so tightly stitched into place that it felt like an old leather shoe that has become wet then left to dry stiff and hard in the sun. Its muscles had stopped working. Here she was a thirty-seven-year-old housewife unable to pass water. She wanted to disown her body. She felt foolish, helpless as if she was inhabiting a baby's body. Except that any baby was born being able to do what she couldn't. Babies came into the world screaming anger, wetting themselves freely. Emily could do neither.

Before Emily had gone to sleep Mrs. Schoenburg, the afternoon nurse, a soft-spoken motherly woman, had brought Emily new painkillers, two round green pills. She took the pills eagerly. Her stitches were hurting and the tube the doctor had inserted through her stomach wall into her bladder was uncomfortable. The tube had a miniature white plastic tap on it as tiny as one on a dollhouse sink. The other end was connected to a plastic canteen, a Uripac, into which her bladder was emptied.

Mrs. Schoenburg emptied the afternoon's urine into the stainless steel kidney pan, poured it into a pitcher, then wrote 800 cc's on the record sheet.

"That's only 800 cc's for the day." She frowned.

"But I drank five cups of tea, four glasses of juice and two cups of coffee and it was emptied this morning!"

"Ah well. Never mind," Mrs. Schoenburg consoled her. "Perhaps the morning nurse forgot to put down her entry." She checked the record sheet. "Yes, that's right. There's nothing down for this morning. That accounts for it."

Mrs. Schoenburg reached over and switched off the light.

"Do you think I'll be able to go tomorrow?" Emily's voice was wistful.

Mrs. Schoenburg patted her arm comfortingly. "It's early yet. Usually it takes a week or two to get going. Every woman's different. Some women are tricklers going a little more each day until they're back to normal. Other women are gushers: They just pass water all of a sudden. My guess is you'll be that kind, though it's hard to say. The important thing is to push fluids and relax. That's the secret. Now you get some sleep. "

EMILY'S HALLUCINATIONS began with the night light, an orange cube recessed into the wall at the foot of her bed. When she came out of sleep, her eyes focussed on the orange cube. It glowed queerly in the dark. Emily blinked. The orange light sparked, flickered, became two. Emily closed her eyes. She heard a rush of whirling air near the door. She blinked again and saw something dark by the wall, something that whirled and spun like a top, an elongated top, a column, a pillar of black mummy-bandages. As it whirled closer the bandages unwrapped themselves, lengthening, snapping off ceilings and walls. The mummy whirled around the foot of the bed then veered toward the window, spinning. Suddenly it tilted itself and came straight toward Emily, there was no mistaking its intent, its attack on her. Its orange eyes narrowed to glowing slits, its black bandages flapped across her feet, her legs, her chest then up to her face slapping at her nose, her mouth, smothering her. Emily's hands went up to tear them away. She opened her mouth to scream, to protest, to breathe. No sound came out.

The white arc of light swept across the bed, incurious, routine. Emily sat up in its glare shaking her head to free herself, pawing the air. Her chest was heaving, sweat was running down her back. Thin strips of black snaked around her arms.

"A bad dream?" the night nurse asked from the doorway. Her voice was hollow like it was coming through a long metal tube.

"Not a bad dream. It was worse than that. It was an hallucination. I think," Emily said slowly. "It was terrifying."

The night nurse didn't ask for details but kept the flashlight trained on Emily's face. All Emily could see of her was a low stocky shape blocking the doorway.

"It must have been the green pills," Emily went on. "They must have caused it."

Still the night nurse stayed where she was; one of her hands holding the door open, the other the flashlight.

Emily wanted to shout, "Get that light off my face!"

But she couldn't say it, just as she'd been unable to scream.

"I'll make a note of it on your chart," the night nurse said and, snapping off the flashlight, went out the door leaving it ajar.

A corridor of yellow light, shining water, open sunny fields shone bright and warm beyond the door. Emily kept her eyes on the warm light listening for sounds: the ringing phone, tapping oxfords, murmuring voices: the nursing station was right across from her room. Finally as she was sliding into sleep, gently this time, a narrow letter being eased into a wide envelope, she heard a voice. It seemed to be coming from a valley far away past the fields and shining water.

"Miss-us," the voice called, plaintive, needing rescue, "Miss-us."

It was the old Italian lady two doors away in 310, six weeks in hospital with a gall bladder operation. Emily heard her every night calling the nurses: she never used the buzzer. Sometimes she called for an hour before the night nurse finally went to her.

In the morning Emily drank a glass of juice, a glass of milk and two cups of coffee from her breakfast tray. After she had bathed and powdered herself, she pinned the offending Uripac to the inside of her nightgown where it didn't show except as an unnatural bulge on her hip. She imagined she resembled a diseased tree whose trunk was distended, the sort she saw in front of people's houses, varnished and hung with signs and lamps. Emily thought they made obscene use of deformity.

She went into the corridor, crossed to the kitchenette, opened the fridge and forced down two glasses of apple juice. Then she began to walk. Down one side of the wing past bare walls painted buttercup yellow, across the end of the corridor where the colour changed to turquoise, then along the other wing where the walls were bubble gum pink. The colours were so determinedly cheerful, so garishly bright, they looked like they had been chosen from a package of Easter egg dye. Although the floors were unblemished by scuffs or stains, a uniformed man was buffing the shining tiles with an electric polisher. He kept his head down, avoiding the string of women trailing past. One woman, a day out of a hysterectomy, staggered past, pale, unsteady, holding onto her metal intravenous stand for support. Clear fluid dripped down a tube into her arm; she looked like a prisoner of war surrendering to some ingenious method of water torture. Other women, three or four days out of surgery, walked gingerly, one hand on the corridor railings, the other holding their stomachs. Some women managed to do this unobtrusively as if they were merely intent on keeping a hand pocketed: others were more careless, beyond modesty, boldly pushing hands against their incisions.

Though her stitches pulled, Emily walked straight, hands at her sides. She walked and walked, stopping at the end of the corridor where there was a large picture window. Sealed behind the glass she heard no outside noises, saw no sign of movement except smoke from chimneys curling upward toward the low forehead of winter sky. The city was locked in white Siberian silence, in square straight bars of concrete, plate glass and pavement. Emily kept walking. Until she thought the morning fluids had worked themselves into her bladder. Until she felt the urge to have a bowel movement. That was important, Mrs. Schoenburg had said, some women went by doing the two together.

EMILY WAS SITTING ON THE TOILET with a magazine propped up on top of the disposal can, reading, trying to keep her mind off going. The tap was carefully adjusted to simulate a gentle flow of water, a small brook falling over stones. In Emily's lap was a basin of warm water in which she held her hands. She couldn't figure out why keeping her hands in warm water should induce the urge to go but it did. She felt her bladder muscles pull in slightly. But the sensation was so weak that it had no effect. She tried to relax by forming a mental picture of herself as a sleek jet flying at cruising speed, moving effortlessly through the air, coming in for a landing, coasting onto the runway, stopping, opening up the baggage compartment, the suitcases dropping out, one by one.

She had a bowel movement but no urine came with it. The bathroom had a rich fecund smell that was comforting. At home she used Pine Fresh to get rid of the odour but since being in the hospital she'd grown more appreciative of the powerful smell of her own feces. She was reassured by it like a baby proudly filling its diapers.

The door burst open abruptly almost knocking the basin of water off Emily's knees. A fat arm reached in, jerked up the lid of the disposal tin, yanked out the white plastic liner and pulled the bag through the crack in the door. The magazine fell to the floor. Emily couldn't bend over to pick it up. There was no point anyway. The woman would be back again with a new plastic liner. There was also no point in resenting the intrusion. There were no secrets in this ward: sanitary napkins hung in gunny sacks on doors, enema syringes and douches were thrown into wastebaskets for visitors to see, nurses and nurses' aides burst into the room without knocking, bringing in clean sheets, thermometers, catheters, medication, meal trays, water jugs. It was the same with the housekeepers. They started in the corridor at seven in the morning and kept coming into the room in erratic thrusts of energy: to dust, to mop, to clean the bathroom sink, disinfect the toilet bowl, empty the disposal can.

Both the housekeeper's arms and legs came into the bathroom this time as a new plastic bag was inserted into the disposal can. Emily recognized the fat limbs as belonging to Jessie. It was Jessie's voice she heard every morning outside her door first and loudest. Grousing about the nurses. What they expected. It wasn't her job to pick up dirty laundry. It wasn't her job to carry out meal trays. Those nurses were always trying to get you to do work for them. You had to stand up to them, that's what you had to do.

Jessie disappeared again. Emily stood up, added more hot water to the basin, picked up the magazine, sat down and concentrated on choosing something to read. Most of the articles were about women who seemed freer than herself: Do-It-Yourself-Divorces, The Advantages of Being Bisexual, Adoption for Singles, even the titles depressed her. She was so far behind the times, there seemed no hope of her catching up or even understanding what was going on.

The bathroom door was flung open again and there was Jessie in full glory, her fatness encased in a mint green uniform, her frizzy hair framing puttyish skin. Jessie shoved her mop between Emily's legs. Or tried to. Emily resisted. The least the woman could do was ask her to move her feet.

Jessie poked the mop under the sink, whanging it roughly against the tiles.

"You still on the can?" She grinned raw friendliness at Emily, showing a wide ban of purplish gums above her dentures.

Emily nodded but kept her eyes on the magazine.

Jessie tilted her head to one side and leaned on the mop bunching up her heavy breast.

"Tried beer yet?"

Emily looked up. "Why? Is beer supposed to work?"

"Work! I'll say it works! Some of them younger doctors prescribe it. Maybe your doctor don't know about it."

"You can't have beer in the hospital."

"Ha! That's what you think. I know two women down in chronic keep wine in their closets. You can bet your bottom dollar their doctors know about it. There was a woman here last month in the same fix as you. She had beer." Jessie leaned over conspiratorially. "Kept it in her shower."

That would be a good place to keep it all right. Emily wasn't allowed showers yet so the plastic curtain remained closed.

"See what's good about beer," Jessie went on, "is it goes right through you so fast. Works like a charm."

"Maybe I should try it. I've tried everything else."

"That's the spirit. You get your hubby to bring you some beer next time he comes and you'll pee all right." Jessie stabbed the corner with the mop then closed the bathroom door, satisfied. Emily could hear her in the bedroom banging the mop against the baseboards, the closet door, the waste can.

LENA WHYNAUGHT WAS a big bold girl who was Emily's seatmate in Grade Three at Harbour Mines Elementary back when there were two to a desk. Lena lived in a shack on the outskirts of town with nine other kids and smelled stale as if she ate, slept and played inside a breadbox. In November Lena came to school with impetigo: yellow oozing crusted sores spotting her arms and legs. She was sent home and never came back. But before she left, she sat through one of Miss Frazee's lessons on manners. Halfway through the lesson, Lena put up her hand.

"Please, Miss, I got to pee."

Miss Frazee suspended the chalk over the blackboard where she had been writing down different ways of answering the telephone. She smiled encouragingly.

"That's not what we say, Lena."

Lena put a hand to her crotch.

"Please, Miss, I got to piss."

The smile remained fixed.

"What we say, Lena, is we have to go to the bathroom."

Even toilet wasn't good enough for Miss Frazee. An English teacher, Miss Frazee constantly exhorted them to refine their speech. The English language must not be corrupted with vulgarisms.

"But we have a privy, Miss!" Lena said, looking around the class, enjoying the audience.

Only then did the chalk touch the blackboard, the smile disappear.

"All right, Lena. You may go. I'll see you after school."

The Grade Two teacher, Mrs. Fairweather, had made them hold up either one finger or two and say aloud number one or number two. Emily didn't know why it mattered for the whole class to know which you had to do until Squirt Layton told her. If you put up two fingers Miss Fairweather didn't question how long you were gone from class whereas you were allowed only five minutes for one finger. Most of the boys said number two until Miss Fairweather caught on and questioned them closely in front of everybody, threatening to write notes home to parents, making sure the big jobs, as she called them, were done at home.

The nurses called it passing water, the doctor voiding. Emily's husband, Don, said taking a leak and crap. When they were younger, her children said wee-wee and poop. Since then Emily had taught them to say urinate and B.M. She had taught school herself, social studies, so she had more leeway than Miss Frazee. Emily was no longer sure of these words. Choosing the right word had become important to her. She had the idea that if she came upon a certain arrangement of words, it would have the power of a chant and the muscles of her bladder would magically open like the doors of Ali

Baba's cave. She remembered how effective schoolground chants were in exorcising tattlers.

Tattle-tale tattle-tale
Tie you on the bull's tail.
When the bull begins to pee
We will have a cup of tea.

Jody Strom was a little girl who used to play with Emily's ten-year-old daughter, Megan. Until Emily caught her with her pants down defecating under the spruce tree on the front lawn. When Emily asked her what she thought she was doing, Jody simply pulled up her pants and walked home leaving Emily staring down at droppings lined up like a row of sausages in front of the tree. No dog would do that. The child must want attention. She'd better tell Marg Strom. Since the divorce Marg had gone back to university to study social work. She was away all day. Jody must be trying to tell her mother something.

Emily waited until she thought Jody would be in bed before she crossed the street. Through the window she could see books and papers spread over the kitchen table. Marg came to the door wearing reading glasses.

Emily tried to be brief.

"I hate to bother you, Marg, but I think you should know that Jody's been defecating on our front lawn. Judging from the number of droppings it looks like she's been doing it for a couple of weeks." Emily felt this was a reasonable beginning: a statement of fact.

But Marg was annoyed. "Come off it, Em. Did you come all the way over here to tell me about a few turds? I've got a term paper due tomorrow."

"Well, if it was my daughter doing it, I'd want to be told."

Emily didn't know why she felt it necessary to explain this.

"You and I are different. I don't let details like that bother me. I've got better things to do with my time."

Emily wasn't about to let this pass.

"Perhaps you'd better spend more time with your daughter instead of at the university. I mean it is social work you're taking, isn't it? What better place to start than at home!" The bandages flew out of Emily's mouth like tongues of fire. "Maybe you should take the time to see what your daughter's done to our lawn. And when you come, bring a shovel!"

After she had stormed home, Emily felt terrible to have said so much or to have said it the wrong way. There were two other children besides Jody. It must be hard raising them alone. The next morning she went to the florist and bought a white rose in a bud vase, getting Megan to take it over, to show Marg she was sorry. Marg never acknowledged it. Which Emily took as further proof of her failure to speak her mind without going too far.

It had reached the point where she would avoid making a complaint even when it was justified. She did this with her family: day after day she picked up dirty clothes, wet towels, newspapers, wiped up spilled milk and mud tracked as far as bedrooms, saying nothing. There was no one around to say anything to anyway, they were all off to work or school when she set to cleaning up, muttering, shaking her head. Then one day she would burst open angrily: the whole family—Don, Tom, Megan, Jimmy—came under fire. She overstated her case, played the martyr, exaggerated the wrongs until she became disgusted by her dramatization, her inability to be casual and matter-of-fact.

"Maybe you should go back teaching," Don said to her after one of these sessions. "I don't think you're cut out to stay home."

Contrite, determined to reform, to become the all-giving earth mother, Emily would scrape off Don's windshield, start the car for him, pick up the children's clothes, take out the garbage, begin the cycle all over again.

EMILY HAD BEEN DRINKING BEER for two days averaging three bottles a day. She had one after her nap, taking the bottle with her into the sitz bath. She ran two inches of water as hot as she could stand and sat in it drinking beer. The idea according to the nurses was to pass water in water. To Emily this was tantamount to going in the sea. She tried to recall those lazy summer days as a child when she lay like a fish in a tidal pool at Ingonish. She leaned back in the bath, closed her eyes, the beer making her light-headed, and tried to hypnotize herself into thinking she was a fish that rested in the shallows, the fluids of its body moving with the tide. It didn't work.

She had another beer with Don during evening visiting hours. After he had left she tried to squeeze in another. It was really too much. One night, a Saturday after Don had gone home early to watch the hockey game, Emily took a bottle of beer with her into Gina's room. She had taken to visiting the old lady in the evening, thinking if she got more attention she'd be less likely to call out during the night. Whenever she visited Gina, Emily took something with her: a flower, a chocolate bar, a magazine.

The first time Emily went into Gina's room she'd been appalled by its starkness. When she walked past other rooms she saw bouquets of flowers lined up on windowsills: roses, mums, carnations done up with ferns and bows. There were boxes of chocolates, books, magazines, and always a new pastel-coloured bathrobe folded across the foot of the bed. The old lady had nothing. Except for the empty water glass on the night table and the woman herself sitting in the corner chair with a blanket over her knees to cover up what the blue hospital gown did not, the room might have been unoccupied. Gina had the abundant white hair and brown eyes of a defeated matriarch. Even the sagging tea-coloured jowls couldn't disguise the strong cheekbones, the thrusting jaw. There was no smile whenever Emily entered the room, only a nodded acknowledgement that another brief distraction had come her way like the feather of a migrating bird fluttering into her lap.

Tonight when she came into the room, Emily asked the old lady if she would help her out by drinking some of her beer.

"I like wine, Missus," Gina said, "but I take beer."

Emily poured a glass full of beer and handed it to the old lady who took it with a firm hand.

"How's it going tonight?" Emily said.

"Terrible. The doctor says I go home tomorrow."

"Why that's wonderful."

Gina took a swallow of beer and eyed Emily balefully.

"Maybe for you. Not for me. My husband have bad heart. Can't help me to bathroom. My son works."

"Isn't there someone who could help you, a V.O.N. nurse?"

"Maybe. I like to get woman in but my son won't pay. He wants me to cook for him. I'm not wife. Too old. He should get wife. He stay with us because he wants house. My husband and him build it a long time ago. When my husband die, my son put me in place for old people." Gina shook her head. "In Italy my mother turn over in grave."

Despite or maybe because of Gina's pessimism, Emily couldn't resist the urge to patronize.

"I'm sure once you get home, things will work out for the best."

"Maybe Missus," Gina said sourly, "maybe." She finished the beer and held the empty glass up for Emily. Emily took the glass to the bathroom, rinsed it out and brought it back three-quarters full of water. The old woman waved it away.

"Is there anything I can do for you before I go?"

"No, Missus. No," Gina said. "Nothing."

Her sad eyes dropped to her lap. Emily's visit was no more, no less than she'd expected.

EMILY HAD BEEN IN BED AN HOUR staring into the dark. As usual her door had been left ajar. But the corridor of yellow light no longer shone bright and warm beyond her door. She could hear a storm: Chill laughter and word gusts coming from the nursing station. She remembered it was Saturday: the nurses must be having a party. She got up, unpinned her Uripac from the bed and padded across the bare floor to the door.

"Missus! Missus! I need you!" With all the commotion in the nursing station Gina's plaintive voice might have been coming from the bottom of an abandoned well.

"Missus! Come quick! I need you."

Obviously no one was going to help the old lady. Emily put on her slippers and padded down to 310. When she pushed open the door, Gina whined, "Oh Missus, you came. I got to go bad," and assuming Emily was the night nurse, said, "That lady, she gave me beer."

"I'm not the nurse. I can't take you," Emily said, "but I'll ring for someone."

She went over to the bed and pushed the buzzer.

The old woman grabbed hold of Emily's arm. Emily tried to pull away but the grip tightened as Gina began to lever herself up with Emily's arm.

"Please Missus. You take me. That night nurse mean. She won't come. She hates me."

Emily jerked away.

"No! I can't lift you or I'll pull my stitches. I'll go up to the desk and get you a nurse."

When she stood in the doorway of the nursing station, simply stood there until the laughter subsided and they noticed her, she was aware how strange she must look, at least to herself if not to them. They were used to women whose nightgowns were hitched up by plastic tubes exposing white legs and shaved public hair. One of the nurses came forward and Emily knew by the stocky shape of her that she was the night nurse. She was unprepared for the youngness of the face, the childish snub nose, the wide flatness of the eyes. She didn't look mean or hateful, only untouched by experience.

"The old lady in 310 needs to go to the toilet," Emily told her.

"She's always saying that," the night nurse said. "When we get her up, she doesn't go. Later she wets the bed."

"I'm sure that happens," Emily conceded, "but the fact is she definitely has to go now."

She didn't stop there. She knew they might think she was interfering but she didn't care. She was going to say it anyway. She looked at the night nurse. "You know," she said, "it wouldn't hurt to remind yourself that you might be eighty-four someday and needing attention."

Then she stomped across the hall, got into bed and went to sleep.

TWO HOURS LATER her bladder woke her up. The sensation to go was so strong she got up too quickly and was pulled back by the tube pinned to the bed. She bumped into the night table. It banged against the wall. Fumbling with the pin she tried to free herself. She couldn't manage it. She yanked the tube clear, disconnecting the Uripac from her bladder. Not bothering to turn on the light, she followed the well-worn path to the bathroom. As she was settling onto the toilet she kicked over an empty beer bottle she'd forgotten to put back in the shower. It clattered into the corner.

The night nurse opened the bathroom door and shone the flashlight on Emily's face.

"I heard banging. Are you all right?"

"Of course I'm all right," Emily said. "And don't shine that flashlight in my face."

The flashlight beam swung to the floor and circled the bottle.

"It looks like you've been drinking," the night nurse said.

"That's right," Emily said triumphantly. "And I'm peeing too."

"You're what?"

"I'm PEEING!" Emily shouted it out. *Open Sesame*. The proud rush of yellow fluid came warm between her legs.

Mrs. Schoenburg had been bang on: she was a gusher all right.

Batter My Heart

LYNN COADY

YOU SEE IT THERE, every time on the way back to the old man's. Put up by Baptists or the like, about twenty miles or so from the toll booths. What always happens is that you go away and you forget that it's there until the next time. Just when the fog and eternal drizzle have seeped deep enough inside your head and sufficiently dampened your thinking, it leaps out from the grey and yellow landscape—the same landscape that has been unravelling in front of your eyes for the last three hours. Lurid, oversized letters painted with green and red and black:

Prepare

To Meet

THY GOD

Then the bus zips past almost before you can be startled. And it makes you smile for a moment, just like it always has, and then you forget about it, until, presumably, the next time you've gone away and then come back again.

By the time it gets dark, you are driving through Monastery, so called because there is a monastery. You know when you're passing it because there is a large cross lit up by spotlights positioned on either side of the turnoff. Earlier in the day, the driver slowed down and the people oohed and pointed because a small (it looked small, in the distance) brown bear was scampering toward the woods. Just before disappearing, it turned around to glare. These are all the signs.

The monastery you remember from twice in your life. Once, a pious little kid with your family. You saw the crosses marking the graves of dead monks, you saw the building but didn't go inside that day. It hadn't looked like a monastery. Industrial, like a hospital or a prison. It had been built sometime in the fifties. You drank water from a blessed stream.

Now they run some kind of detox program there, the drunks living with the monks.

The second time, you were a less-than-pious teenager there to visit both your boyfriend and your history teacher. The two of them were actually related somehow—same last name. He had told you it was a disease which runs in his family. The history teacher, far worse than him, older, having had more time to perfect his craft. The monastery like a second home. Word was, this time it was because he had showed up at an end-of-the-year staff party at the principal's house and walked directly through a sliding glass door. He had a PhD and spoke fluent Russian.

You walked into the common room with your boyfriend and the history teacher was sitting at a table playing gin rummy (ha, ha, ha) with the other drunks. You and he chatted a moment, he condescending, as usual. But not nearly so much as when he was drunk. You can't remember why, but the last thing he said was that you would never make it in the big world. You could only agree, pliant. You still agree. What did that mean, though, make it? Did he think you would shrivel up like an unwatered plant? But at the time, you didn't care, you didn't care to defend yourself, you didn't care about any of it. It was liberating, that. It was almost fun. All of a sudden you didn't have to be nice to the boyfriend who used to seem so sad and fragile, who used to get drunk and then go and take a dirty steak knife from out of the dishpan and look at it.

NOW ABOUT DADDY, different people have said different things. He is the kindest man you could ever know. Well—he's got his own way. He's got his own opinions and goddamnit, he's not afraid to express them. With his fists if it comes down to that. Quite the temper. Quite the mouth, if you get him going. A good man. The only honest man in town. A visionary. A saint. Would do anything for you, but if you disappoint him, I guess he'll let you know it. Stark raving mad. One mean son of a bitch.

You get home, and Daddy's throwing a man off of the step.

"Mr. Leary, I implore you." The man is filthy, flabby, pale.

"Get offa my step, you goddamn drunk."

"Mr. Leary, I've changed. I've turned over a new jesus leaf."

"And what d'y'know, there's a bottle of Hermit underneath it!" (A sometime wit, Dad.) "You're more full of shit than my own arse. I'm through wasting time with you, Martin. Offa my step."

"Another chance, Mr. Leary, that's all I ask." The bum straightens himself with boozy dignity.

The old fella has caught sight of you. "Hello, Katey! Martin, I'm telling you for the last time to fuck off. I won't have my little girl gazing on the likes of you."

Martin turns, he seems to bow, but may have just lost his balance. "Hello, dear. I'm sorry not to have a hat to tip at you."

Daddy steps forward with a no-nonsense air. His fists are clenched, his jaw is clenched. It should be laughable in a man this side of sixty, but here is the truth: he is terrifying.

"I'm not gonna tell you again." His voice breaks a little, as though any minute he's going to lose control. Again, it seems so put on that it should be ridiculous. You would think that, anyway. Martin is no fool. He retreats into the driveway.

"Mr. Leary," the bum says, actually resting his hand on his heart. "You were my last hope. I went around tellin' everybody who would listen, Jane at the hospital and them, I ain't worried, no matter how down I get, I know I can count on Mr. Leary to come through for me."

"Don't you try to make me feel guilty, you sick bastard!" Daddy shouts. "I broke my ass for you, Martin, I put my ass on the line!" But Martin is stumbling down the driveway. He has his pride.

"Jesus bum." Dad looks like he wants to hit something. He always looks like that. "Come in and have a bit of tea, now, Katherine."

Daddy had done all he could for Martin. This is what you hear over tea and bannock and cheddar. Put his ass on the line. Tried to get him straightened up. On his Jesus feet again. Martin lived in an old pulp-cutter's shack out in the woods with no water or electricity. His wife dead of a ruined liver. Both boys in jail for the drunk driving. His girl off living with someone. Dad spits, sickened.

Dad normally wouldn't have done a blessed thing for the drunken idiot, but there had been something rather enchanting about him when they had met over the summer. "Lyrical," Daddy says around a mouthful of bannock, surprising you with the word. Daddy had been on the river helping out a friend with his gaspereaux catch. This was etiquette—everyone who had a fish trap helped everyone else load their vats. Daddy didn't begrudge his friend this, particularly because his own catch, brought in last week, had been larger.

Dad had been sitting on the edge of the trap once the last vat was filled, wiping sweat from his pink, hairless forehead, when Martin Carlyle appeared from out of nowhere and greeted him. The two men had never actually come face to face before, but, as both had attained a kind of notoriety within the community, they recognized one another, and each knew the other's name. Now Daddy puts on a show, acting out the two parts:

"Good day, Mr. Leary, sir!"

"Hullo, Martin."

"By the Lord Jesus, it's a beautiful day!"

"Yes."

"Did you catch a lot of fish today?"

"One or two, Martin, one or two," Dad says, squinting up at the man, who has a terrible matted beard and pee stains on the front of his pants.

Now Martin stands in silence, weaving just a little bit, and appears to be thinking very deeply about something.

"Mr. Leary," he says at last, "I put it to you. Would this not be the perfect day to be bobbing along down the river in one of those vats with a big blonde in one hand and a bottle of Captain Morgan in the other and a pink ribbon tied around your pinocchio?"

Daddy concludes the performance, sputtering bannock crumbs from his laughter. "Lyrical," he says. "That's what you would call lyrical, isn't it, Katey?"

THERE YOU WERE IN THE MONASTERY, once upon a time, a walking sin.

Defiling the floor tile upon which you tread. A sin taking life in your gut. No one can see it, which is good. Being a girl is bad enough, in a monastery. The drunks turn and stare.

Martin Carlyle among them at the time. A pink ribbon tied around his pinocchio. Sitting on the bridge that crosses the blessed stream as you and the boyfriend traipse by along the muddy path. Spring. Grimy, miserable season. You irreverently spit your gum out into an oncoming mud puddle, and he shoots you a dirty look. Impiety. He's religious now, after two weeks among them. Martin is on the bridge with a fishing pole between his legs. He calls:

"Hey-ho, Stephen, boy!"

"Martin!" Raises his hand.

"Whee-hoo! You got a little friend!"

"How are you, Martin?"

"Ready to break into the vestry, that's how. Get meself a little taste of wine!"

"Don't do that, Martin, don't do that now."

"No...."

Together, you walk up the hill to look at the stations of the cross. He is insistent that you pause at every station. The women clamour at the feet of the suffering Christ. He keeps telling you about how different he is. He keeps saying things like: "I pray now. I honestly pray." And, "Everything seems right. Like all my problems were meaningless."

And you say: "Of course it does," and he says, "What?" and you say, "You get to be in a monastery."

He tells you, "The monastery doesn't have anything to do with it. You just have to learn to pray. I mean really pray. What that means is accepting God."

Well, you are certainly too much of a hardened and worldly-wise seventeen-year-old to go for that. "No way," you say.

"Why?" He gives you a gentle look, and you see that he thinks he is a monk. Wise, wizened. Sleeping in a narrow bed, in a little cell, humble. But when you spit your gum out onto the path, and were impolite to Brother Mike, he wanted to hit you. You could see that. Any fool could see that.

"Nothing to accept," you say.

"You can't believe that." Misguided woman. Is there no one left to condemn you? No one, Lord. Then I will condemn you.

"Belief," you say, "doesn't come into it."

He attempts to look at peace with himself yet disappointed with you all at once. Then: "Do you want to go see the shrine to the Virgin?"

Why not? Very nice, very pretty. Easily the prettiest thing here in man-land, white stones and plastic flowers all about. He tries to hold your hand, to create some kind of moment, sinner and saviour. He looks over: "Do you want to kneel?"

"No, I don't want to kneel!"

HE SMILES when you leave, all benevolence, alongside of his favourite monk, Brother Mike. He had wanted you to talk to Brother Mike for some reason, but you said no. He was disappointed, but he said he understood. He thinks that you're making the wrong decision, going away, but he understands that too. He understands everything. He and the monk stand side by side waving goodbye. When you first arrived, it was Brother Mike who intercepted you. You had gone into the chapel instead of the main entrance, and stood overwhelmed by the height of the ceiling, the lit candles, the looming statues of saints looking down from every corner, the darkness. For want of something to do while you waited for someone to come and find you, you went over and lit a candle for your dead Gramma.

Brother Mike had been kneeling up front, but you didn't even see him because it was so dark. He was standing right beside you before you noticed him. He spoke in a natural speaking voice, not a whisper, which in a church seemed abnormal. "Are you Katherine?"

He led you to the common room, and that was when, watching your feet hit the grey industrial floor tile, it occurred to you what a desecration your presence constituted. Every heartbeat, every snoutful of sanctified oxygen you took went blasphemously down into your bellyful of sin to give it strength.

Brother Mike looks around to see if you are still following and gives you a kindly smile.

"Well, the boy had a lot of anger when he came here. A good deal of anger with himself and the world. I think you'll see a big difference."

Now, a few years gone by, the phone will ring late at night. Not often, but every now and again. Bitch. Heartless, stupid.... Just like old times!

THE DAY AFTER YOU ARRIVE is Sunday, and it is clear that he expects you to accompany your mother to church. No argument. My, hasn't Katey changed. Because then, it used to seem like there was some kind of moral imperative to jump up and down on the backs of their sacred cows. Isn't it, you used to argue into Daddy's pulsating face, more of a sin for me to be sitting there thinking the whole proceeding is a pile of shit, than for me to just stay at home? And now you don't care if it is or not, sins and moral imperatives alike being figments of the past.

But when the choir isn't present, ruining the peace, church can be nice, the sun coming in through the fragmented window. You can sit alone among everybody, enjoying your mild hangover. Everybody murmuring responses to the priest in unison. You do it too and are not even aware. That's nice. The powdery smell of clean old men and old ladies all around. The feel of their dry hands when it comes time to extend the blessing to one another. You love the sight of old men in glasses, kneeling, fingering their beads.

But one of the last times you were to mass, also sixteen, Mommy insisted for some reason on going to the early one and there you are with the worst hangover in the world. Ever, in the world. Mother, God love her, with no idea. You say in the car: Hm, Mom, I'm not feeling so good this morning. She says: Yes, Margaret-Ann's kids are all coming down with the flu.

Inside, everything makes you nauseous. You remember that your Gramma had this bottle of perfume that she only wore on Sundays, for mass. She said that she had been using the same bottle for thirty years, and only on Sundays and for weddings and for funerals. You remember that because it smells like the old women sitting on all sides of you must do that, too—don thirty-year-old scent for mass. Everything smells putrid. You think that the old man in the pew ahead must have pissed himself a little, as old men will. The priest waves around incense. You stand up, you sit down, you stand up, you sit down, you mutter the response to the priest. You turn to tell your mother that you need to go outside for air—dang flu bug. Halfway down the aisle, bile fills your cheeks.

Outside, you run around to the back of the church where no one will see you because it faces the water. It's February, the puddle steams. Your breath steams. You eat some snow and gaze out at the frozen strait, mist hanging above it. Hm, you think.

Today, it's not like that. You feel pleasant, dozy, as soon as you take a seat beside your mother in the pew. You pick up the *Catholic Book of Worship* and read the words to the songs. You've always done that, ever since you were small.

Sadly, the choir will be singing today. The well-to-do matrons with sprayed silver hair and chunky gold jewellery. Most of them are members of the Ladies' Auxiliary. You don't know what that is. Mrs. Tamara Cameron approaches the microphone and tells everybody that the opening hymn will be "Seek Ye First." This is the one where they all try to harmonize one long, high-pitched "ALLLLL-LEEEEE-LOOOOO-YAAAAA" with a whole verse. They think it sounds ethereal. The organist is a stiff, skinny fifteen-year-old outcast who appears to be scared out of her mind. You lean over to ask Mommy where the real organist is, Mrs. Fougere, who has been there for as long as you can remember, and your mother whispers that she is dead, as of only two weeks ago.

The first chord that the fifteen-year-old hits is off-key, causing Mrs. Cameron to glower. The girl is going to cry, maybe. No—the song begins.

The congregation has always liked the choir because it means they don't have to sing. They are content to stand there, holding their books open in front of them. But Mommy always sings, choir or no, and she holds her book at an angle so that you can see the words and sing too.

A wonderful thing happens, now. You notice Martin Carlyle, shuffling unobtrusively into the back row of the choir box. He is wearing the same clothes you saw him in yesterday. He blows his nose quietly, with deference, into a repulsive piece of cloth and then tucks it back into his sleeve, where he got it. He picks up a hymn-book, flips it open to the correct page after peeking at someone else's, and decides to join in on the high-pitched "Alleluia" rather than the regular verse. Except that his voice isn't high-pitched, like the ladies'.

> Seek ye first the kingdom of God
> And his righteousness
> And all these things will be offered unto you
> Allelu, alleluia

Mommy says into your ear, "There's Martin," unsurprised, which must mean he shows up for this every Sunday. That is why Mrs. Cameron has failed to glower, and only looks a little put out. What can she say? They are all God's children.

AFTER YOU'VE BEEN AROUND for a while, Martin seems to

turn up everywhere. He's the town drunk, is why, and the town is small. Every Sunday, you see him at church, singing in the choir, his voice even more off-note than the ladies'. Half the time he doesn't even know the words and sort of yah-yahs his way through. One day you do an experiment and go to the nine o'clock mass instead of the later one. There Martin is, singing away.

He never recognizes you, even after the time on the step. One time you see him at the bar bumming drinks and you are so pissed that you say to the assholes you are with: Look! It's my soul-mate, and you go over and fling your arms around him and call for two scotches and sodas. You remember him blinking at you with reservation and saying, Thank you, dear. Thank you, Miss.

Another day you go to the bar—even though you have been saying to yourself all along: I probably shouldn't go to the bar—and of course on that day you see him there and he comes and sits down at the table you're at. So then you go and sit down at a different one but then he comes and sits down there too. All he does is look at you and smoke. It is the first time you've been face to face in two years. At a third table, he sits down right beside you and tells you, in a number of ways, that you are a terrible person and why. The assholes you are with examine their drinks. If one of them would at least move, you could get up from the table.

FOR A LONG TIME, nothing much happens.

THEN, WORD COMES AROUND that Martin has shot himself in the head. Doctor Bernie, a second cousin, calls from the hospital and informs Daddy that the patient has been asking for him.

"Holy shit!" says Dad.

"Yes," the doctor replies. He has an implacable, sing-song voice which has always annoyed you and your father equally. "He's been asking for you ever since they brought him in here, Alec."

"Well, holy shit, Bernie, is he going to live or what?"

"Oh yes, he's sitting up having a cup of tea."

Dad has to get you to drive him to the hospital because he is "so Jesus pissed off I can't see straight."

"Holy shit," he keeps muttering, and, "Stupid bugger."

In the hospital, you hang around the reception desk listening to his voice resound in the corridor. It is a small hospital. Nurses rush past to silence him, not understanding that their pasty, wrinkled faces and harsh, hushed voices and fingers pressed against their lipless mouths are just going to make him angrier. You remember this from all your life. Shrinking down in the front seat of the car while Daddy yells at a careless driver. Shrinking down in the wooden desk while Daddy yells at your math teacher. Shrinking down into the chesterfield while Daddy yells at the television. Everything making him angrier and angrier and nobody getting it right.

But when Daddy emerges, trailing flustered and ignored nurses, he is laughing.

"Leave it to Martin," he says. "Shoots himself through the head and even that doesn't do him a bit of good."

"So are you going to help him again, Daddy?"

"Well, Jesus Christ, Katey, what are you gonna do, you know?"

HE DOESN'T REALLY KNOW what to do anymore, he's done so much already. He used to drive Martin to A A meetings (much as he had hated them himself in the old days) but was soon informed by such-and-such that Martin took advantage of the trips into town to visit the liquor store and drop in at Buddy's Tavern. And everything ended up like that. Daddy had badgered social services into boosting Martin's allowance so that he could buy some soap and deodorant and Aqua-Velva and clothes to get himself cleaned up for the job Dad had managed to get him sweeping up at the mill. Then, when Dad heard about the new public housing units that were going up, social services found themselves duly annoyed into putting one aside for Martin, even though they were being clamoured for by single mothers and the like.

So Daddy drove out to Martin's shack in the woods that had no water or electricity, and laid all of this at his feet.

"By God, Martin," he said, "you'll get the new place all snugged up nice and pretty soon you'll be having your daughter over for Sunday dinner."

"No, Mr. Leary, my daughter wouldn't come over so she could spit on me."

"Well, goddamnit, you can have me over to dinner!"

"Proud to, Mr. Leary."

Daddy handed him the keys and, looking around at the differing piles of junk that served as Martin's furniture, told him to just give social services a call once he got everything packed away and ready to go. They'd come and get him moved in. "By the Jesus, I'll come and help too," he added.

"God bless you, Mr. Leary."

"Aw, well, what the fuck."

Dad left, feeling good, stepping over Martin's sick, emaciated dog, King.

But the months went by and social services called up—Mr. Leary, there is a list of people as long as my arm who are waiting to get into that unit, and it just sitting there.... Dad barks something that shuts the sarcastic little bastard right up, and then hangs up so he can phone his buddy at the mill. How has Martin been getting along? Martin Carlyle? He didn't show up, Alec, and I wasn't expecting him to.

Outside of the shack with no water or electricity, Daddy found Martin asleep on the ground while King sniffed daintily at the surrounding vomit. Martin's drinking friend, Alistair, was leaning against the side of the house taking in the sunshine. A beautiful spring day. He was not passed out, but cradled a near-empty bottle of White Shark against his crotch, serene and Buddha-like. He squinted up at Daddy and said that himself and Martin had been having "a regular ceilidh" all month long with the extra welfare that Martin was now getting. Daddy kicked the dog into the woods and threw the bottle of White Shark in after it. This having been the incident that preceded the throwing of Martin Carlyle from Alec Leary's step, where you came in.

DADDY HAS A SORE KNEE. It makes him hobble when he walks, and it makes him angry. You have to go out and help him bring the wood in because none of your brothers are about. If you were one of them, it would be a bonding moment between you and him. It might be anyway. He likes you when you work. Here is one thing you know: Men love work. You might not know anything about what women love, but men love work.

You can always tell when it's Martin phoning, because Daddy's tone will become reserved. You hear him say things like: Well, I'll do what I can, Martin, but I'm not making any promises, you hear me? I can't just give give give. Then Dad will hang up and turn to you.

"If that Martin Carlyle ever comes around when I'm not here, don't you let him in."

"No."

"Do you know what he looks like?"

"Yes, I've seen him a million...."

"A big fat hairy ugly bastard and he's got a hole in his head"— Daddy points to a spot above one of his eyebrows—"where the bullet went in."

Daddy is busy these days with the Little League. The head of the recreation department called him up and asked him to coach.

"Nobody else wanted to do it, I suppose," he grunted into the phone. "Selfish whores."

And your mother, observing that you never seem to go out anymore and have absolutely nothing to occupy your time, ever-so-delicately suggests that it would be nice and he would like it if you attended the games. So you do, even though you have no understanding of baseball and don't know when to cheer or when to boo and are the only woman there who isn't somebody's mother and almost get hit on the head with a foul ball twice. You watch him hobbling back and forth in front of the dugout, hollering at both teams and causing the little guy at bat's knees to knock together. At the end of every game, win or lose, he takes them to the Dairy Queen and buys them all sundaes. You get to come along, too. You have coffee. The little boys look at you and ask you questions about yourself. Are you married? What grade are you in? They can't quite figure out where you fit. You answer every question as honestly as you can, but it doesn't help them any.

Soon, you're attending the practices, too. Maybe you are the unofficial mascot. Dad gets frustrated with them one day and steps up to the plate to show them how it's done. He can't throw anymore because his arm cramps up when he raises it above his shoulder, and he can't run because of his knee, but he gets the best pitcher on the team to throw him one so they can see how to hit. The clenched fists and clenched jaw all over again—overweight, balding man clutching a child's tool in his large, pink hands. When he swings the bat, it makes a sound that frightens you and you look up from picking at your nails and see that all the little round faces are turned upward in awe.

Circle

SHERRY D. RAMSEY

FOR MOST OF MY LIFE I've wanted to believe in extraterrestrial life. And I don't just mean bacteria, I mean a full-blown civilization of space-faring aliens. The tiny office in my farmhouse has a poster on one wall, a collage of fuzzy photos; mystical black discs and blips and indistinct spheres, and the word "BELIEVE" stark across the bottom. My kids think it's weird and cool and funny, the same way they think about me, I guess. That's how most kids see their Moms.

I wanted these aliens to be the kind who'd come to earth on a mission of mercy, saving us from ourselves, showing us how to cure the world's ills and making us do it. God knew the people who currently ran the planet weren't going to. The job needed someone with a higher motivation than greed, power, or narcissism.

I wanted aliens who would come and threaten humanity, if necessary, into doing the right thing.

I didn't expect miracles. Aliens wouldn't resurrect my long dead father, or find and rehabilitate my despised absentee ex-husband. They wouldn't make my mortgage payments or put my kids through college. But they could make starvation a thing of the past, depose tyrannical governments. Disarm nuclear weapons. Cure cancer and AIDS. The big things.

My office window looked over the farmyard, where I could watch the chickens and the dogs and cats and sometimes my kids or the hired men. It was like spying on a microcosmic world, and sometimes I'd jot down story ideas when I was supposed to be doing the farm records. Occasionally I'd show them to my daughter Sal, who'd read them gravely and say something like, "That's cool, Mom," with the seriousness that only an eleven-year-old girl can summon.

Once in a while, late at night, when the farm records were finished, I'd actually work on a story, the house quiet and comforting around me. The office was my sanctuary, and the word on the poster was my mantra.

I did want to believe. But wanting something doesn't make it so, and I had come to the reluctant conclusion that I didn't. And because I didn't believe, I didn't hope, and since I didn't hope, I was sad that summer.

It had been a good planting season. Spring arrived early, with warm soft rain and sunlit skies and no late frosts. By mid-July the corn was a foot over my head, the ears beginning to swell with the promise of sweet cream-and-yellow kernels. I made the rounds of the fields every day, although I knew the hired men took good care of the crops. I'd fired hands before if they were slack, and jobs were scarce, and my men were aware of both facts.

But I liked to keep up my presence in the fields, even at this time of year when there wasn't much to do except irrigation and pest control.

I keep two horses, and preferred to take one of them on my rounds instead of the truck or the scooter. I really can't afford them. I keep telling myself it's good for the kids to have the horses around, but Duke and Jen are really there for me. I just can't justify the expense any other way.

This particular morning I had saddled up Duke and headed out to what we called the "back" field, furthest out from the farmhouse and closest to the mountain that reared its evergreen head in the northern distance. It was a typical hot July day, and I'd passed the irrigation trucks working the closest fields first. As I swung Duke down the familiar trail, through the thinly wooded copse that separated the back field, I grinned. I like being the first one to walk the land in the morning. It seems somehow more proprietary than just dropping in later to check on the hands.

We emerged from the copse at the crest of a slight rise, the corrugated rows of corn sloping down and away from us. A breeze blew down from the mountain, setting the tufted stalks waving like hands, and for a few moments I just let my eye sweep the vista, feeling proud and possessive and lonely.

If it hadn't been for that breeze I might have missed it, might have turned Duke away and headed down the western path to sweep around the perimeter, check the fence and then go home. But because I paused on the crest, watching the undulations of those uniform rows, I noticed the spot that did not move.

And once I had seen it, I had to know why.

It was near the center of the field, maybe a little to the left. I rode Duke down the path as close as I could and dismounted. He couldn't thread his bulk through the thick cornstalk forest without leaving a swath of destruction in his wake, so I looped his reins over the rail and gave him a pat. Then I ducked into the corn.

If I had been walking north, along the direction of the drills, it would have been easy to keep to a straight path, but cutting crosswise the plants are not so evenly or uniformly spaced. I could see the summit of the mountain if I craned my neck, so I used that to get my bearings. The corn rustled and hissed around me, sharing secrets the wind had whispered as it passed.

Then the rows ahead thinned and opened out and suddenly I was standing at the edge of a wide compass of broken and battered cornstalks.

"Dammit," I said, my voice small and lost in the corn's rustling. At first I could see nothing but the damage, the loss in dollars and cents. Who would do such a senseless thing? I stood glaring at the stubble, silently demanding that it name its attackers.

And then it registered that the damaged patch was a circle. A perfect circle of wilting stalks stencilled into the greenery of the field.

Automatically I looked up. Foolish, I know, but who had not

heard of, seen aerial photos of, the mysterious and sensational crop circles? Hailed by the tabloids as hard evidence of alien visitation, studied by believers and unbelievers alike, explained away by various, numerous, not-quite-good-enough alternate theories.

The sky was azure, serene, and empty, of course. I quickly looked back down at the damage, glad there was no one about to witness the hot flush that mounted my cheeks. For a moment I stood indecisive, then set out to examine my personal crop circle.

It was roughly twenty feet in diameter, as I paced it off. The corn was not burned or seared, but bent, flattened, mostly broken. Three deeper indentations were evenly spaced around the circle's circumference. At each of these, the cornstalks had been cleanly sheared off, and the earth was pressed down in the shape of a crescent, about three feet across.

Somehow, it was those indentations that did it to me. By the time I had decided they were identical my stomach lurched with an unmistakable lifted churning, and I had to kneel in the stubble and press my head to my knees to keep my breakfast down. The battered stalks and leaves were brittle and sharp under my knees and palms, but it didn't matter. Whatever else happened in the future, I didn't want anyone scraping up my vomit for further examination.

When I could move again, I did the first thing that came into my head. I stood up as much of the broken and bent corn as I could, leaning some against the unbroken stalks at the perimeter, balancing other sheaves against each other. My sole thought was that no one else should find this, should see it, until I had thought about it for a while. I didn't want my fields overrun with tabloid journalists and wackos, didn't want my kids turned into freaks on the evening news, above all didn't want anyone to see the circle and then see the poster in my office.

When I had done the best I could, I threaded my way back to Duke, who stamped a foot in irritation at being left alone for so long. The wind had died down and the corn stood silent, hiding its wounds. From the crest of the rise I didn't think the circle was noticeable now, not to anyone else.

On my way back to the house, I stopped and told the men in the irrigation truck that the back field was all right for today, and they needn't water it. In fact, I said, they could take the afternoon off; it was going to be a hot one and I knew they could use a break. They were surprised, but not terribly. I expected, and got, hard work, but I was not an exacting boss.

I went home and thought about the circle while I did the chores around the farmhouse, listened to my kids' stories from school, and fixed supper. In the back of my mind the whole time, the corn whispered and buzzed, telling secrets I could not understand.

THAT NIGHT I DREAMED OF ALIENS. In the dream they emerged from the corn at night, typically slightly built, big-headed, staring with dark, pupil-less eyes. In the yellow light of the back porch bulb I could see that they breathed through a pair of holes at the base of the neck. Fringes of skin around the holes fluttered slightly with each breath.

Still dreaming, I watched them from my office window as they roamed the yard, examining sleeping chickens and scooping up samples of the dirt, plucking blades of grass. They glanced my way from time to time, aware of my presence. The darkened house around me echoed with the sounds of my sleeping children's breathing. I was thrilled and terrified at once. I wanted to go out to them, but I didn't want them anywhere near the kids.

When one mounted the back step and stretched a spindle-fingered hand toward the door, I jerked awake.

It was dawn, and my room glowed a comfortable golden-rose. I got up and padded softly to each of the kids' rooms. There is no denying the maternal instinct that says, "Go check on the kids." The boys snored gently in their bunks. Sal had kicked off all the covers again, and I tucked them around her.

Downstairs, I opened the back door and stepped out onto the porch, enjoying that shivery early-morning freshness that too soon evaporates in the day's heat. I caught myself checking the scuffed dirt for unusual footprints, scanning the yard for anything out of place. Of course there was nothing.

Once the kids had left to catch their bus, I saddled up Jen this time and reined her toward the back field. I told myself that all I would find would be the same mess I had left yesterday, broken and battered cornstalks lurching crazily against each other, if they hadn't all toppled down overnight. But I had to go.

I knew the spot where I had left Duke and now left Jen there, ground-tied so she could busy herself with the succulent grass. She'd be less impatient if she were eating.

Again the mountain was my guide, and in some places, my faint trail from yesterday. When I broke out into the circle, I saw what I had tried to convince myself I would not see.

The corn was flattened anew. Three new indentations marked the ambit of the circle.

I stood and stared. *Believe.* Could I? Because if I wanted to so badly, why was I still not convinced? Why did all those other explanations, formerly so inadequate, keep flashing across my mind?

Again I tried to right the stalks, to create some illusion that nothing was wrong here. It was more difficult today. More stalks were broken, and they were yellower, more brittle. I did the best I could, but the camouflage didn't work nearly so well. I still had no plan.

I was threading my way back to Jen, the broad, rough corn leaves catching at my clothes, when I heard a truck engine drawing nearer. The irrigation truck! They'd be doing the back field first today, since they'd skipped it yesterday. Standing in the back of the truck, someone was bound to notice. I couldn't just send them away. After yesterday it would seem too strange.

I grabbed Jen's reins and led her up the trail, thinking quickly. When the truck drew into sight, I sighed with relief. Only one man in the cab. There'd be one in the back, too. But if I could get rid of one of them, I could replace the man in back and work the irrigator myself, while the other drove the truck. Chances were the driver wouldn't notice anything.

I waved to them, and the truck stopped. I led Jen up to the cab and said to the driver, "Charlie, I'm glad to see you."

The second man, Wilt, clambered down out of the back of the truck. "Got a problem, Miss Jill?"

Don't ask me why Wilt insisted on calling me that. Most of the men just called me "Jill," some of the younger ones made it "Miz Landry." I kind of liked it, though, and it hurt to lie to him.

"I think Jen's bruised herself," I said, stroking her nose. "She seems off in the left fore, but it comes and goes. Would you lead her on back home? I'll work the back."

Wilt nodded, but Charlie looked doubtful. "You drive, Jill, and I'll work the back. It's heavy work with the hoses."

I smiled. "That's all right. I've done it lots of times before, you know that. It'll make a nice change. Seems I spend too much time in that office these days. The sunshine'll do me good."

And they couldn't really argue more than that. I was the boss, after all. From my perch in the back of the truck I could see the circle plainly, a yellowing wound in the green skin of the field. How long could I hide it?

BY THAT AFTERNOON I'D DECIDED. I still didn't believe, but I wanted to, and I would give myself one more chance. It felt like a lot was riding on it.

I got Ellie Small from down the road to come and stay with the kids for the night, saying I'd gotten a call from an old friend who want- ed to meet me in Searsborough, about twenty miles away. I might not want to drive back alone if it was late, I explained, and Ellie clucked and said it was no trouble. I could tell from her voice she was hoping the "old friend" was a man, and I let her think so. Ellie's a sweetheart.

So I made a pretense of getting dressed up a little and heading out in the pickup, where I'd already hidden a change of clothes and my sleeping bag. *I'm only going to do this once,* I told myself, *and that's it. Aliens, if you can hear me, you've got one chance to show yourselves.*

I did drive into Searsborough, maybe to ease my guilty conscience a little, and had supper and did a little shopping. I bought treats for the kids, because they'd be hoping, although they'd never ask. When it was good and dark, I drove back home, left the truck on the side road, changed in the cab, and cut through the woods to the back field.

It was nighttime quiet, which is hardly quiet at all, what with the crickets and an occasional owl and the small rustlings in the underbrush, but quiet compared to the daytime. The sky was patchy with clouds, but they were drifting slowly, and sometimes the moon would show through the gaps like a glowing nickel cut cleanly in half. I swore under my breath for forgetting a groundsheet, and spread my sleeping bag out on the already dew-damp ground at the crest of the rise, just inside the treeline. I didn't expect to sleep.

For a long time I sat with my back against a slim white birch, thinking about what I'd do tomorrow. Whatever happened tonight, I couldn't let anyone else find out about the circle. So I thought about that, and about the farm, and about what a jerk my ex-husband had turned out to be, and how much I loved my kids, and I guess somewhere along the line I fell asleep.

THE ALIENS WERE BACK IN MY DREAM, but this time I was outside with them, far from the sanctuary of my office. We were in the field, and again they came out of the corn, but behind them, through the mesh of broad leaves and stalks, I could see the dark shadow of their ship, pressing down, down into the earth.

This time I could hear the soft sucking noise that emerged from their fringed neck holes when they breathed, could smell the surprising cinnamon-toast odor of their skin. They came up to me where I sat, dream-paralyzed, but not so afraid this time. I knew my children were safe, far away and safe.

They looked at me the way they had looked at the chickens in my other dream, although they made no attempt to touch me. Their eyes, up close, had discernible pupils a shade darker than the surrounding sclera. That made them less frightening. I thought that if I were around them long enough, I'd learn to read things in those strange eyes.

I struggled to speak to them, but in the manner of dreams and nightmares, I was mute. I wanted to ask them, *Why, why are you here? Are you going to help us at all?* I felt sick with the inability to ask them my questions, tell them the reasons I'd wanted to believe for so long, the only things I thought really mattered.

One of them picked up the flaccid end of my sleeping bag, examining the fabric, then let it drop and looked up suddenly.

Following his gaze, I saw that the sky had darkened, storm clouds springing up without warning in the manner of hot summers, and realized that the wind had freshened, sweeping down from the mountain with rain on its breath. A sucking roar filled the trees overhead.

ABRUPTLY I WAS AWAKE, sputtering in the downpour that took only seconds to soak through my sleeping bag. The wind howled through the corn now, whipping the tufted stalks into a mad dance, bending them nearly double.

I struggled to my feet, tripped on the sodden sleeping bag and stumbled against the birch. *Damn, damn.* All for nothing, and now I was soaked to the bone. I turned to make my way back to the truck, thankful that the wind would be behind me most of the way.

Then I heard it. It rose as only a low purring over the sound of the wind, although it would have seemed loud on a calm night. I whirled back to the cornfield, sickly certain I'd see a dark, rounded shadow rising over the lashing crops.

I did.

Anger boiled up through me, warming me despite the chilling rain. I shook a fist at the slowly ascending sphere.

"Why?" I screamed, but the wind tore at my voice and scattered it through the forest. "Why didn't you answer my questions? Why the hell are you here?"

The black sphere made no reply as it rose higher, toward the barrier of dark cloud that would be no barrier to it. My chest was heaving, but I felt like I could barely breathe. Tears coursed down my cheeks, indistinguishable from the rain.

Curiosity. The word brushed my mind like a butterfly, out of place in my wild, jumbled thoughts. I jumped as if someone had spoken behind me.

Like you watch things out your window.

The ship continued to rise, betraying nothing, a dark shadow against the dark sky. My knees buckled and I sank down to kneel on the drenched sleeping bag. The wind was the sound of my children's breathing, close in my ears no matter where I was.

"I watch the things I care about," I heard myself saying in a small voice. "I watch what I love."

You use it to understand the world.

Confused, I could think of no reply.

We don't understand your world. Yet. But when we do, we'll help if we can.

And then the shadow was melting into the churning mass of clouds, and rising up toward the other side where the moon still shone, silver and placid in the night sky above the storm. The last word brushed my mind like the ghost of a prayer.

Believe.

THE STORM HAD ABATED and the sky was lightening by the time I made it back to the truck, dragging my leaden and probably ruined sleeping bag. I climbed thankfully into the cab, and stared at my pallid face in the rearview mirror while I wiped it dry with a half-clean rag from the glove box. It looked unfamiliar.

Because I finally believed? In what?

I started the truck and turned it off the road, bumping slowly over the terrain until I drew close to the back field's eastern fence. I clambered up on to the roof of the cab to get my bearings, and could just make out the dark shadow that was the circle.

Then I aimed my truck at the fence, gunned the engine, and gave it hell-for-leather.

The fence thudded flat and I bounced into the cornfield, gritting my teeth as I mowed down stalk after stalk of my summer's profits. When I came to the circle I slowed a little, making sure I ran straight through it, then spun the wheel and whipped around the perimeter, churning up corn and earth into an unrecognizable mess. Then I straightened out, put the pedal down, and charged out the other side of the field, broke through the fence there, and didn't stop until I fetched up beside the road to Searsborough.

As I bumped over the shoulder and headed for Searsborough, my face was wet again.

WHEN I DROVE INTO THE YARD much later that morning, dry and clean and with the truck sparkling, Charlie met me with a grave face.

"We had some damage last night, Jill," he said, shaking his head. "Must have been some young bucks out on a tear. Bust right through the back field fence, skidded around her for a while, and *Bam!* out through the other side."

"Oh, Charlie!"

It was a relief to let the night's anguish into my voice. I'd fought it down, kept my head while I did what had to be done, but now my hands and voice shook. Charlie read it his way.

"Didn't lose the whole field, though," he said quickly. "Just a strip through the centre, really. Hard to say the cost. Might not be too bad."

Tears stung my eyes at his sturdy optimism. I turned away quickly, drew a deep breath. Charlie took my arm.

"Well," I said, "it could have been worse, I guess. All a part of farming, sometimes, taking a loss."

"All a part of life, Jill," Charlie amended, and I had to agree.

SO NOW, I BELIEVE. But I'm left still wanting to believe, too. That they'll learn what they need to, and that they'll help when they can.

I hope it's true. And I pray it's soon.

Overburden

D. C. TROICUK

GOD FASHIONED THE FIRST MAN out of the dust of Eden. But there exists a breed of man made of a blacker dust than this, the dust of eons ago, though it was not dust then, but a murky oblivion that time compressed into solid night. The men who descend daily to those sunken remains of primeval forest feel it still. The overburden that transformed it transforms them. This is a breed of man neither born of woman nor made by God in a single day, but formed by the unceasing oppression of the tons of earth and ocean water upon the ceiling of his heart. He is a man such as this one who stands staring down into the small fire burning in his kitchen stove.

Roddie MacSween sifted through these ideas, his thoughts not phrased nearly so eloquently as he believed the poetic images deserved. He was a smart man, quick with concrete information, awkward when it came to concepts and emotions. A man of few and simple words, he could rarely do justice to the complex impressions that swarmed in on him at times like this when the constant accusing voice inside him stilled and the feelings were all he had.

He rubbed his cold morning hands, blue-veined and arthritic, one over the other. The bed of kindling ignited a shovelful of coal at its dusty perimeter, sending up a sulfurous smell. In minutes, energy subdued for a thousand years within a five-foot seam of black ore would be released as heat to this chilly September day.

Roddie MacSween—Doc, they called him—did not enter this

world as black dust any more than Adam had entered as clay. But black dust was what he became. Day in, day out, for twenty-two years he had ingested the dust for lunch with Kam sandwiches and Maple Leaf cookies. He drank it with cold, over-sweet tea from a mickey bottle that fit with a flat-curved neatness into the back pocket of his work pants. He inhaled it with every breath until, like the prehistoric seam he worked, he slowly petrified into a creature of the mine, his lungs encrusted, his heart hard and dark with a hidden anger that released, when it did, in a slow, hot burn. The dust ground into his pores, branding ownership with blue scars on his hands, at his temple, in places people never saw. Once he had driven a pick-axe through his left foot and there, he supposed, the dust had penetrated his ruptured cells because after that, he noticed, even to the naked eye his own blood sample looked darker than the others going for testing.

And yet, after the years he had considered utter misery, years that had gone by like eons, he missed the routine of the mine. Some days he believed he would trade his remaining days on earth for one last ride to hell—down the rake with his buddies, forty minutes of vulgar camaraderie over a hand of Tarabish, forty minutes stolen out of the shift by travel time to the wall face where they worked the seam.

That daily ride, the human contact of it, had become even more significant when he became Deputy Mine Examiner. Most of his duties sent him into virtual isolation to pace off the miles of ordered underground roadway as he inspected for safety hazards and air quality. He knew the caverns of the north wall complex as well as the upstairs hall of his own house yet his eyes, craving substance, searched the darkness ahead for some reference point, and his mind, never quite convinced that the next intersection was not a turn into oblivion, charted his progress on a mental map. Before passing through each wooden air trap, he chalked his initials and the date on the man-door, a procedure that was as official as a notary's seal in the event of an accident. It indicated the last time the area had been examined and by whom. But for Doc it was a validation. I was here, therefore I am. He stepped through, needing a conscious reminder that the barrier had been erected, not to conceal some subterranean Black Hole, but to redirect maximum ventilation to the areas where men were currently working. The lamp on his hard hat showed him the way, but his way was always and only a tangible void, a black tunnel at the end of the light.

THE WAR HAD CLARIFIED the vague, juvenile image he had of himself. He now saw himself involved in some kind of healing occupation: male nurse, physiotherapist, something that would sterilize the gangrenous souvenirs his mind had picked up in the mud and trenches. Fresh back from Europe, recovered from a foolish barracks accident but unscathed by the enemy, he had openly bragged about his three-year stint as a medic, but never spoke of the risks—to the lives of those he had saved, to his own future career, the risks of performing procedures he was not qualified to tackle.

The same young women who had once ignored him listened, rapt and silent, as he embellished accounts of gruesome operations undertaken in impossible conditions, and of the miraculous recoveries which had followed. He had never thought past a hospital job before, but the new attention made him cocky, and after a month home he had set his sights on the top of that pyramid of medical professions.

His father had other plans.

He was lucky to get on at Caledonia, lucky to get work at all. They all told him. He knew it himself. So each day, trying to be grateful for his meagre pay until the fall term at Dalhousie, he donned the same filthy pit clothes he had worn yesterday and descended the deep. And if those dreams of becoming a doctor were like heaven to him, then that place warmed from the molten core of the earth could only be the first step to hell.

The analogy was amusing at first. When he could still see it as a temporary arrangement. During that time it was the dream that drove him, made him survive it. But before long it seemed irreverent to even take the dream down there with him where no living thing could take root. Instead, he sent it up on the wash-house hook with his day pants and shirt and there, untended, that living flower of hope withered. As airy and frivolous as a dandelion gone to seed, it waited for the merest breath of wind to dissolve completely.

HIS RETIREMENT ROUTINE had evolved to this: tend the garden, read the paper, drive Theresa to the mall. While she scouted for the ultimate bargain, he methodically paced off the enclosure of the mall, the same room-and-pillar formation he knew from the mine, one long central corridor with parallel side tunnels shooting off in either direction. Mentally he chalked the perpendicular passageways, the click of his cane on the terrazzo floor drawing him into the past, stirring up the questions of a young man, now old, whose dreams had been thwarted.

Mickey Porter elbowed him in the ribs. "If life's a bowl o' cherries, b'y, then what'm I doin' in the pit?"

Doc swung around, dodging the image of hands groping for him from out of some unearthly darkness. A shiver shocked his body, the impression still fresh of blue-black bodies that had raced through his sleep again last night. They were not night-dwellers, these, but cried out from his stream of consciousness at every turn. He would like to have believed they were nameless, faceless spectres, but he knew. He knew who they were, knew them by name, knew their families. He saw them in the eyes of their fathers, their brothers, their sons. He rarely met those eyes anymore. More than he feared his own death he dreaded the stiletto death wish in their warm hellos, the slash of violent reproach in their passing nods of greeting.

Some, like Mickey, he knew too well to avoid. They stopped him in the mall to shoot the breeze or tell a joke and, without missing a beat, he would grin and lapse into the local vernacular.

"How she goin, b'y? On the back shift again?"

"Yeah, and can't get a wink of decent sleep," Mickey growled cheerfully. "And you, you got 'er made, you old bastard."

Doc laughed shortly, not fully meeting Mickey's eyes, but glancing there, where the affable ignorance of the role Doc had played reproached him more severely than if the man had placed his large hands about his throat and squeezed until relief came in the form of that other blackness.

Yes, they thought he had it made, retired for seven years already, and only fifty-eight. He had used an old war injury as an excuse to accept a pre-retirement package, not entirely untrue. The doctor had warned him for a long time that his bad knee couldn't take the punishment. In the last couple of years the Official's cane he used to sound the stone roof provided an additional support on his rounds of the north wall, a necessary insurance against those times when the knee gave without warning.

Mickey called him back to the reality of the Mayflower Mall.

"Hey, b'y, you with me or against me?"

"I was just thinking...."

"I tried that once. Hurt like hell."

They were silent for a minute, watching the people pass.

"Seven years today, Doc."

Mickey let the words slip out of him, natural as breathing, a soft echo of the phrase that had been passing through Doc's mind all morning. He did not need a calendar to place the date. In his mind, a year was a circle starting and ending at this point. The cycle of his life revolved in sync with it.

"He woulda been thirty-four next month, my boy."

Doc nodded. "I'm sorry, Mickey. Maybe I...if I could've done it different...."

A tide whose period was twelve months, one that had come seven times now, surged against his throat, threatening to swallow him up and drown him.

Mickey gave him a reassuring slap on his back. "Nobody coulda done nothin', Doc. But thanks."

He dampened a flare of anger at Mickey's ignorant forgiveness.

"It was my wall," Doc said.

Mickey shrugged uncomfortably. "How were you supposed to know?"

"It was my job to know," Doc snapped. "It was my job to—"

The temperature was rising, the mall closing in. Above him a skylight admitted full, bright sun, but around the perimeter of his vision the light was failing. Figures who, a moment ago, were strolling the mall now seemed to be coming at him from all directions, bursting into the closing lens of consciousness, all with accusing faces, with eyes that knew what Mickey Porter did not.

He made for a nearby bench protected from the glorious sunlight by a net of ficus branches. Embarrassed by his weakness, he fiddled with his cane. Through the roar in his ears he could clearly distinguish the unyielding tap of its copper tip sounding the terrazzo.

THE DEPUTY'S CANE, his own cane, rapped the cement floor of the wash-house. Doc tripped up a ginger tabby, one of several cats that came every night looking for scraps. He flung it aside with his boot.

The manager and clerk were waiting grim-faced, warned by the staccato click. When Doc had no time for the strays, something had to be up.

Doc set down the Clanney—the lamp whose flame was an omen he read like a mystic reading an oracle. He knew what Frank thought, that it was as accurate as a crystal ball. He felt the burn of ridicule along his back as he scratched his report into the book with a dull pencil, anticipating his defense, reviewing the facts in his mind.

In the presence of methane gas, a slender yellow sheath encompasses the normal blue naphtha flame inside the Clanney's glass case. The height of the sheath indicates the percentage of gas. But it is not merely the presence of gas that creates the danger. It is the ratio of methane to oxygen that is critical. There must be sufficient oxygen to feed the explosion, enough gas to fuel it. When seven to fifteen percent of the air is composed of methane, an explosion that could be measured on the Richter Scale might be initiated by an action as incidental as the spark of metal scraped on metal. A concentration as low as two percent signalled conditions dangerous enough to evacuate the mine.

Today, almost one-half inch of yellow surged up from the burning blue bud. No, the measurement wasn't scientific, not like the new electronic sensor they were coming out with. But Doc wasn't sure he could trust a gadget that acted without an innate regard for human life.

"You gotta shut 'er down, Frank," he said with resolve as he turned around.

Frank nudged Dannie, the clerk. "Get me that report, will you?"

Dannie sidled away, reluctantly accepting the bogus dismissal.

"I can't do that, Doc, and you know it."

"One and three-quarters, Frank," he stated solemnly.

He was referring to the percentage of the lethal methane gas. It was as close to the limit as he had ever seen. And it scared the hell out of him.

Unmoved, Frank walked over, nudged the report book toward Doc. "Kenny'll open a few traps, clear it out."

Doc tapped the pencil, staring him down.

"We lost two days' production last week from that pan-line breakdown," Frank said. "You rather be responsible for four hundred men on the welfare when the company shuts 'er down for good? 'Cause that's what they're gonna do if we don't keep production up."

They heard a file drawer close and Dannie shuffling restlessly about in the inner office.

"Let's keep that just between you and me, for now." Frank nodded conspiratorially, with an affected look of concern for the common good.

Doc could second-guess Frank, but he didn't know for sure. Of four mines, this was the last left in town. The others had closed when the proportion of work-hours to travel time became unprofitable, when two hours or more were spent getting each shift of men from the surface to the workable coal face. But who knew what other criteria management used, what production quotas they required?

Doc pictured the line of faces that had passed down the rake with him that morning—Sam, supporting both mothers-in-law; Reggie with nine kids under the age of eleven; John R. whose house burned to the ground last winter, and no insurance; every one of them with his own tale of woe. He reached for the pencil and swore to God this would be the last time he would give in to that bastard. Somehow, next time he would dig deeper, find that place in his heart where courage and youthful dreams were stored together.

"So, are we shutting down or what?" Dannie wanted to know.

"Nah!" Frank guffawed. Taking the pencil from Doc's hand, he pressed the lead firmly into the tiny dot, embedding it into the page. "Doc put the decimal point in the wrong place, that's all."

Desperation saturated every pore as Doc scrubbed the coal dust off his body that day. More worn and raw then he'd been in years, he emerged from the wash-house a wounded animal and returned home to bleed anger into the family. Theresa herself, made over-sensitive by a separate issue with her sister, retaliated with such a vengeance that Doc slunk away ashamed, knowing she should have been the balm that soothed him, knowing it was his own fault that she had never been that to him.

Later, he found her in bed, crying. She hadn't done that since she went through the change. He turned to her, a darker form against a dark pillow, wanting to vent his rage, not at her, but with her. But how could he say the things he wanted to without making himself party to the conspiracy? He should have stood up for what he believed. He should have told them. He should have at least told her.

A RARE TORRENT OF EMOTION raged through his veins, a flash flood that filled him to bursting. He remembered a strong young man who had helped save the civilized world, who, if he had not always acted with courage, had returned from the war charged with it.

That was what he was feeling. Recognition of it spurred him to action. He cursed the hour that prevented it, and settled for resolution.

By God, he would do it. Tomorrow. Walk into the office, right up to Frank's ugly face, and tell him he had endangered the lives of his buddies for the last time.

He smiled in the midnight gloom, savoring the sound in his mind. *Buddy.* More than a pal, a miner's buddy was a lifeline, a saviour if the situation called for it. They were the men who shared together the darkest places imaginable, as if the tunnels they burrowed together opened parallel passageways into their own souls. As if in the sharing of their daily tasks they touched together some Ultimate Truth that no outsider could ever hope to comprehend.

The burden on his heart eased. He reached for Theresa's hand. Her fingers, lying outside the blankets, were cold, tense, but waiting. He held on, tightly, all the will of his heart expressing itself in his touch. Without a word, her hand gradually warmed and relaxed and when she turned to come into his arms, he knew the apology was complete.

Tomorrow, then.

DOC WAS WIDE AWAKE at the first blare of the whistle, his chest pounding. He willed it to stop, to be the shift whistle or the double blow to announce that the shift would not work. But it went on and on, an unbearably long, tense wail riding the silent night alerting the town to the emergency.

He pulled on a pair of pants over his pyjama bottoms and was in the pit yard before he realized he was still wearing his corduroy slippers. He burst into the crowded wash-house, grabbed the man nearest the door.

"Where?" The single word was all he could get out.

The man shrugged him off, not hearing over the din.

He asked again, loudly: "Where is it?"

"Four north." The informant eyed him cautiously. "Your wall, ain't it?"

He nodded weakly.

"Musta built up pretty quick."

Again, the faint movement of his head, another acknowledge-ment of the conspiracy to which he was now, irrevocably, a full partner.

It was hours before anything happened.

The first draegermen to come up were assailed by a dozen men in the same breath. "How many?"

They were grim. "Don't know," said one. "Fifteen come up. The ambulance will take the worst, but we could use a hand if any-body knows First Aid."

Bent over an injured man, Doc's medic experience was fresh as all those yesterdays ago. But there was an element missing, some-thing he had once had in the grasp of his heart, but was gone now. He could work no miracles here, only wait helplessly with the others and, from time to time, hold a small paper cup of water to a dying man's lips.

"COME ON, BUDDY, take a drink."

Mickey pressed a styrofoam ridge to Doc's lips. He drank. It was lukewarm tap water, reeking of chlorine. What he needed was a shot of black rum.

He forced himself to swallow.

"I gave them water like that. Just like that. In little paper cups."

Doc talked down the mall, and Mickey looked in that direc-tion. "Who?" he asked, mystified.

"Your boy. The others."

"Jesus, Doc. You still beatin' yourself over the head with that? It was seven years ago, b'y. Let go of it."

Doc shook his head. "I can't," he said hoarsely. "I killed them all, the five of them."

He took another swallow and looked up into Mickey's silent looming presence.

"Get a grip, b'y. Nobody's to blame."

Doc bent his head, slowly shook it, unabsolved. Now, as during the hours of vigil seven years before, he tried to imagine, to put himself underground when it happened. The explosion deep below the surface was not beyond his imagination. Surely it must compare to what happened inside him that night when he had imploded, when he had become what time had made of some ancient forest on this very site eons ago, a shallow blackened thread that once was a man named Roddie MacSween.

*H*ome *F*ires

CAROL BRUNEAU

*O*N TUESDAYS I clean the house top to bottom, whether it needs it or not. I start at the kitchen sink, scrubbing off the tea stains, then work my way upstairs, dusting and scouring. A light sweep of the bedrooms, the parlour—the least-used rooms—saving the bathroom and the blue-stained tub for last. Gives me something to do with the place empty—a body can only bake so many pies and squares and loaves of bread. Then there's Archie's room—he's been gone ten days now. Today I'll give his room a proper going-over, now I'm finally up to it. Figure I'd better make up for all the years I couldn't get past his door, let alone give the place a good scrubbing. If I don't do it now I never will.

The morning he left for Ontario I climbed the attic stairs with the dry mop and started under his bed. Wads of dust like hairballs the cat brings up, grey fur mixed with the sandy strands of Archie's hair. Tied a clean rag over the mop and knocked down the cobwebs hanging like beards from the ceiling. Looked like the room had been vacant for years, though God knows the hours Archie spent holed up in there once he left the garage.

"Why don'tcha go uptown and see what the other fellas are doin'?" I'd ask, but he'd just moan. "Aww, Ma, they're all wrapped up with the girlfriends these days." So I could see he had no interest, no interest at all in his old friends. It was like having a bit of gravel in my shoe, knowing he was up there moping around all day. Not do-

155

ing much of anything besides lolling on the bed with his shoes on, reading magazines, day in and day out. As for the mess in his room—it wasn't that I was slack so much as the fact he was always in it.

Even as he was backing his green Ford onto the road, looking hard into the side mirror with a cigarette clenched in his teeth, I was thinking how I'd go in and get the Mr. Clean and the new yellow bucket hanging in the porch once he was gone. To take my mind off things. Yes, as I stood at the gate waving, waving till my shoulder ached, I was thinking how I'd polish the banister in the hall, wipe down the taps in the bathroom, maybe do under the beds in the boys' old room. Then on to the attic and Archie's den. I had it all planned how I'd go up and sort through his closet, clear out some of the junk. Those greasy black boots from his old job, that boxful of spark plugs and fan belts, the rubber dry and cracked like stretched licorice. I'd take down the faded blue curtains and wash them, run a dust-rag over the baseboards, the windowsill. I was thinking how much bigger the room would look without the clutter as I watched the car burble down the street, picking up speed in front of Pritchard's dairy. *Keep busy, keep busy,* I kept telling myself. It was better than wishing I was in that car too. Like his guardian angel, as the Catholics say. Never mind the boy's nearly twenty-five years old.

In front of Pritchard's Archie slowed down, almost to a stop, and for a minute my heart jumped. Maybe he was changing his mind, deciding Blackett wasn't so dead-end after all. I quit waving, standing there in the dust with my hands folded inside my apron. Praying. But then I saw Pritchards' grandson drag his trike out of Archie's way and over to the dairy steps. I heard Archie honk the horn, just once, and then he was gone. Leaving me with my cleaning, and all the time in the world. Time I would've killed for, other points in my life.

Ten days. The first time I've been alone in this house, not counting those early months Thomas was working double shifts at the bankhead, before my first was born. To me those days don't count, since I was happy enough making his bed and his meals, watching my belly grow. Forty-odd years since Thomas brought me here, a sweet-faced bride. Lordy, I was green! But that soon changed, after the first one came, then the second, and the third—a new one just about every year, nine months to the day after things like Christmas and church picnics. Nine babies in all, not counting two that didn't live. What a woman gets sucked into, having so many kids— your life flies past like a train with no stops when you're used to a full house. Or at least one other body—even if it *is* layin' prone behind a door, no sound but pages flipping.

"Whatcha readin'?" I always asked when Archie came downstairs for more tea or to clean the clinkers out of the stove.

"Nothin' much," he'd say, rooting around the cupboard for a fresh can of milk. I just assumed he was reading about cars, since cars seemed all Archie cared about from the time he could talk. Even his pa—poor Thomas—would laugh and say, "Well, he's a real Cape Bretoner then—got to have a car, never mind if ya don't own a pot to piss in. You can drive a car, Het, but ya can't drive a house." Oh, Thomas used to joke about it, but I don't think he was entirely laughing. Thomas's father was from the mainland, so his people weren't true islanders, not like others around here.

With his love of driving and all, it surprises me Archie stayed home this long. *Lucky to have had him as long as I did,* I think now, as I stand in the pantry working lard into some flour for apple pies, the last thing before I head upstairs. The rolling-pin thuds against the counter, flour dusting the brown painted floorboards. Ten days and not a word, not even one quick phone call. *What, they don't have phones wherever it is you are?* I slice apples for three pies—another church tea-and-sale—though the ladies' auxiliary only asked for one. The dough crusted in my fingernails is a comfort, like the dried-salt tightness of your skin after a dip in the ocean. The comfort of something done a thousand times before. I measure the cinnamon, just enough sugar.

Take it easy, the ladies say. *Have a rest now the young fella's final-*

ly out of yer hair. You got it coming to ya, Hettie. Enjoy the time to yer-self—get out more. Someplace further afield than church or the co-op store. Now the last of yer brood has flown the coop. And not a bit too soon—that last one took some time leaving'.

Truth is, I don't know where to start. When I finish the pies I sweep up the flour, and while they're baking I'll get started on Archie's room. Give it some elbow-grease this time. Because that's what I do Tuesdays. Mondays I do the wash, Tuesdays dust and sweep, Wednesdays scrub, Thursdays bake. Saturdays too, and any other day the need arises. And cook: Friday boiled cod, Sunday a roast of beef, Monday a crock of beans. Even when the others started moving away—all seven boys, before Archie and Grace, my baby—I kept cooking. The same things, just smaller amounts. Using the same old speckled pots, hardly needing to follow a recipe. A lot of it I could've done in my sleep. Till finally Grace said: "You're gonna make me fat, Ma." Archie, though, always appreciated my cooking. Three times a day, on the dot. Archie in his spot beside the window, from the time he was a stick of a thing in the old spool highchair. Lord, it seems just last week I was wiping porridge off his fat fingers and pointy little chin, those wide blue eyes watching me. A grown man now, gone off to look for work the way all his brothers did—out west, all over kingdom come—and Grace down in Halifax with a husband and a baby of her own.

I never thought Arch would leave me. *Not right, a big man like that livin' off his mama.* I know that's what the whole town was thinking, even the clerk in the co-op watching me count out the money for a tin of corned beef, a head of lettuce. For a long time I kept my head bowed, feeling their thoughts jumping like sparks. *Too damned lazy to go out an' support himself. Takin' advantage of his poor mother, an old widow.* As if I had no say in any of it, as if I've gone soft since Thomas died. *Havin' all those kids took the backbone out of 'er. No wonder she's limp as a dishrag, far as the young fella's concerned.*

Soft, *indulgent.* They think I've been too easy on him, that my softness is contagious and Archie's like a cranberry left too long in the bog, deep wine-red but a pulpy mess when you go to pick it. Best left for the birds. *Good for nothin', lazy son-of-a—* But what they don't know is how I've felt seeing so many go. Sure, there's not a mother on this island hasn't had a young one leave for Halifax or Boston, Toronto or the west. And in some ways I wouldn't wish it otherwise. But those other mothers, they act like they're proud. *My girl's workin' for the government now and doin' right good for herself. Yup, the young fella's got a job makin' cars in Oshawa or Windsor, somewheres in Ontario. An' he's got the wife, the kids, a pool in the backyard. Imagine that, now, if ya will.* What they don't say is how they felt the night before, making up a stack of sandwiches, wrapping them just so with wax paper new off the roll, not saved from the day before. Trying to look cheerful and busy, while they're chewing their lips to keep from sobbing.

I've lost seven sons that way, different times. I have a hard time now keeping them separate, remembering exactly who's where, their big ruddy faces all blurred into one. Seven of them, strung all over the country. Gone but for the letters they write, the money they send home at Christmas or my birthday. *Buy yourself something, Ma.* I don't want their money. But I've got quite a pile of crisp new tens in the Pot of Gold box on my dresser. The last couple of years I've dipped into it to send something to Grace for her birthday, or her little girl's, which she always thanks me for. But with fancy little cards, never more than a note.

When Archie was leaving I stuffed a wad in with his sandwiches. I know he would've turned it down if I'd mentioned it. *It's your money, Ma. I don't wanna take it.* Truth is, I wouldn't know where to spend it in this town, except on a card of needles, a packet of hairnets, a plastic rain bonnet, a yard or two of cotton. The only things besides groceries I ever buy. There's not much I need nowadays, at my age. And anyway the bills seem too fresh to spend. Looking at them makes me think of the boys—Fulton, Murdoch, Albert, Donald, Tommy, Dan and Joseph—cashing their paycheques, folding the money into their wallets and setting aside the newest notes for me. But I prefer not to think how they earn them. I nursed Thomas to his deathbed—lung cancer—and he never worked below ground, spent thirty years overseeing the machine shop. Oh, he'd come home a little dusty, but never so's you couldn't recognize him. But no, I can't bear to think of my boys black-faced, nothing but their eyes and the pink of their tongues to mark them from the next fellow, walking hunchbacked the rest of their lives. Like animals, really, tuned to the sounds of water dripping, the darkness of a tomb. But that's how they've chosen to earn their living. And this is why I've never pushed Archie. Not even when people said *Young fella like that, what's he doin' at the garage? Money's a hell of a lot better at the pit.* No, from the minute Archie slid out of me into the doctor's arms, and afterwards gazing into his dark infant eyes, I knew I'd never let my Archie go into the mine.

I untie my apron and start up the steep, narrow stairs, my hand flat against the wainscot to steady myself. At the landing a tiredness comes over me—I realize I've been awake since dawn, for no reason besides habit. I've been trying to sleep more to pass the time. *Relax, relax. Stop wearin' yourself thin. Now's your chance to slow 'er down a bit.* Before I start up the attic stairs I stop at my room and look in, everything neat as a pin. Rankles a bit to think I've *liked* it so tidy: my own little temple, no kids allowed. The way Thomas used to keep me in bed till nearly nine some Saturday mornings, the door locked and the skeleton key on top of the dresser. Lord knows what the boys got into downstairs while we lay there naked, sun blazing around the dark green blind. Before I ever thought of Archie or Grace, my two surprises, one after the other.

Now the whole house is like my room—spotless and orderly as a church, not a thing out of place. Too neat, everywhere but Archie's room. Which is why it's taken me so long to go back up there and finish what I started. Bundle up the magazines for the hospital, see if those fan belts are any good to anybody. Maybe someone could use them. And those old boots. But no, it's early yet to be going through his clothes.

Once I catch my breath I continue upstairs, open the door to the little room. It's cramped and musty, the ceiling sloped over the narrow bed with its sugar-bag quilt, a new sifting of dust on everything. I run a damp rag over the piles of stuff on his dresser, the metal knobs on the bedposts. Grey fluff has started to gather under the bed again—dirt must rise to the top of a house. The air is like cold stew, the dampness drummed in by the mossy patter of rain on the shingles. Shortness of breath makes me sit down hard on the jiggling mattress, and I roll down the sleeves of my work blouse, looking around at the leaf-patterned wallpaper. A stain like a rusty fern has spread under the eaves. Archie could've had the big room next to mine, after Dan and Joe went to British Columbia. But he said he didn't want to disturb me.

I work off my slippers and stretch out, jangling the springs. I try to shut out the gloom, the smell of mildew and rotten wood, a smell it seems no amount of scouring can remove. It was all through the place when Thomas first brought me here from my home by the foundry. After a while it went away—or the smell of diapers covered it up.

I've always hated this house. It's always seemed topsy-turvy, the kitchen at the bottom and the parlour above, like a poor man's idea of something grand. But I never complained. So many stairs, up and down, up and down. No wonder the youngest ones stayed put in the attic—I suppose it was their little refuge, forgotten, at the top of the house. When we came here from the church, my family oohed and aahed about the wide hall upstairs and the polished banister, the deer's head over the coathooks. All except Mama, who sucked in her cheeks and said, "Lord, Lord, girl, all the stairs. Just wait till the babies start coming, you'll be fit to be tied then, Harriet."

As for me, I'd been hoping we'd get to live uptown, in Thomas's family home. The tall green house with the wide veranda, shaded with big heart-shaped leaves in the summertime, a nice barn out back for Thomas to putter. But no. Thomas's sister would have nothing to do with me, and as far as she was concerned it was *her* house, never mind that the old man left it to both of them. And Thomas, God forgive him, wanted to be closer to the pit. *Wouldn't do now, would it, for the men to think I lived up by the bosses?* He thought he was doing me a kindness, too, keeping me close to where I'd grown up. Poor Thomas, as pale a memory now as the foundry. Nothing left but the coke ovens, some brick arches sticking out of the alders, separated from the road by the swamp. *The poison pond,* the boys used to call it when they went down there to visit their granny. *Don't go near it or ya might fall in an' get yer legs burnt off!* I can't remember if it was me started saying that or the boys themselves. And by the time Archie and Grace came along both Mama and Papa were gone, the old house a ruin sagging into the ground, broken windows like empty eyes looking out on the fallen brickwork.

I AWAKE WITH A QUEER JOLT, as if I've fallen from a great height and struck the bed, still holding my dust-rag, not even aware I drifted off. The sound of rain has stopped. I get up and go over to the bureau, lift the pile of magazines to see what's buried beneath. The old tape recorder one of his brothers let him have, a new package of fuses. I set the magazines on the bed, start riffling through them, the glossy pages squeaking between my rough fingers.

Under the shiny covers they're not at all what I expect, which is pictures of cars, things about engines. The only photographs of automobiles are ads—the rest show women, pink-skinned young women in nothing but their underclothes, the curve of a large round breast popping out here, a small pink teat there. They look like dolls to me, plastic bodies too smooth and pink to be real. In spite of myself I turn more pages, faster. The magazine folds open to a woman with hair like yellow cotton candy, wearing nothing at all. I quickly look away, staring at my hands, raw-knuckled against the shiny paper, as if they don't belong to me.

I tuck the magazines carefully under the others and shove the whole works under the bed. I don't know why I'm shaking so, it's not like Archie's a child. I make myself stop long enough to smooth the quilt, slap the pillow into shape. *But he's such a good boy, so serious. Not like some other fellas his age, drinkin' and racin' up and down Main Street with girls snuggled close. No, Archie's too good for such foolishness. Which is why he had to get away.*

If I could just talk to him now, I think, if only he'd phone. It hits me how I haven't grieved like this since I lost Thomas. Not his death—a sting salved with relief—but before that, when I still longed for him the way he once was. A deeper wound, like the mined-out tunnels under the town, emptied, exhausted. The guts of the earth hollow, nothing but a crust of worn-out rock keeping the houses from caving in on themselves.

Gently I shut the door and go downstairs. The fire in the kitchen stove is all but out, rain stinging the windows again. I go to the scuttle in the corner and scrabble for the lumps left at the bottom. But instead of ducking out to the coalshed, I go into the dining room, dim as nightfall though it's not yet noon. I don't bother switching on the lamp, just sit for a while in the little padded rocker. It's cold and damp enough to peel the wallpaper. I pick up the telephone and dial Mrs. Pritchard down the street, the urge to hear another voice swelling like a breaker. *If ya ever need anything,* she's always saying, *if ya ever need anything.* It rings and rings, and after a few seconds I hang up and go over to the fireplace.

Beside the grate is an iron kettle full of shore coal, dull black nuggets like chestnuts. Archie collected it off the beach every time he took a swim last summer, enough for a fire at Christmas and then some. My knees creaking, I kneel on the hearth tiles and begin piling handfuls upon the grate. Once there's a neat mound I get up, my joints cracking with the dampness, and go to the kitchen for matches and yesterday's *Post*, a bit of kindling from the box behind the stove.

I kneel again on the cold tiles, crumpling paper, tucking it into the coal, then strike a match. Light warms the greyness. Flames leap, spreading slowly from the bits of paper to the coal, haloed with pale orange before it burns blue. I squat there, deaf to the pain in my legs. I hold my palms to the screen as brightness fills up the little room, pushing the gloom into the corners. Orange sparks glint in a glass bowl on the table, the rain falling in sheets now at the window, thrumming the garden outside. The coal burns steadily, slowly, a clean blue strength.

I have always loved a fire. It comes back to me how, surrounded by the clamour of children, I could find some quiet gazing into the flames. I could see things—stars. Then somebody would crawl up on my lap or clasp little stick arms around my neck, choking me with hugs. *Watcha lookin' at, Mama? Nothing, oh nothin' a-tall.* They'd look at me worried, the way children do when they sense their mama's not all there. But now there's nobody hanging off my arms or my hips, the flames look exactly as they're meant to, nothing more. I've quit looking for shapes or patterns. I've forgotten about anything more than the feel of dry heat on my face, on my hands, simple comforts.

When finally I let the fire burn down, there are only a few chunks left in the kettle. The clock on the mantel whirrs out three. I poke the ashes, grey lumps which fall into dust. Then I climb the stairs again.

Without looking around, I pull the heavy black tape recorder off Archie's dresser and carry it back down to the dining room. I wipe the dust off, then plug it in and poke around to find the right button. Lord knows what Archie might have recorded—I can't recall him spending much time fussing over tapes. But I keep fumbling with the buttons till I get it working.

The voice jumps out, a cough, a sound like a chair being dragged over crusted snow. *Testing testing, one-two-three-four.* Archie's voice, and then whistling like the hiss of wind through a field of daisies, a tune I recognize. *Yankee doodle went to town a-riding on a po—* Another cough, a long pause, more scraping, then nothing but a furry sound and the little wheels sqeaking around and around and around. I wait and wait for one more word, a whisper, the sound of him breathing. But nothing comes, nothing but the sharp click of the wheels stopping.

The Writers

Carol Bruneau

Though born in Halifax, Carol Bruneau's roots in Sydney Mines, Cape Breton, go back over one hundred years. She continues to spend her summers in Inverness County. Her first collection of linked short stories was *After the Angel Mill*, and a novel will be out in the fall of 2000—both from Cormorant Books.

Joan Clark

Born in Liverpool, Nova Scotia, Joan Clark grew up in Cape Breton and New Brunswick, and now lives in Newfoundland. A widely published author of adult and children's literature, her awards include the Mr. Christie Award for *The Dream Carvers* and the Canadian Authors Association Award for *The Victory of Geraldine Gull*. She is the 1999 recipient of the Mickey Metcalfe Award for a body of children's literature. Her books for adults include *Eiriksdottir, A Tale of Dreams and Luck, From a High Thin Wire*, and *Swimming Toward the Light*.

Lynn Coady

Born in Cape Breton, Lynn Coady is the author of *Strange Heaven*, a novel that has so far garnered the City of Dartmouth Book Award for Fiction, Air Canada's Canadian Author Award, and the Atlantic Booksellers' Choice Award. Her next book, *Play the Monster Blind*, will be published by Doubleday Canada, Spring 2000.

Tricia Fish

Always angry that she was not born here, Tricia Fish lived in Cape Breton from age nine through high school. She is the author of the feature film "The New Waterford Girl." This is her first story in print.

Ellen Frith

Ellen Frith was born in Windsor Mills, Quebec, in 1950. She moved to St. Ann's Bay, Cape Breton, in 1993. She has worked as a journalist, editor, and freelance writer, and her published works include *Rough and Ready Times: The Story of Port Mellon* (1993) and the novel, *Man-S-laughter* (1995).

Claudia Gahlinger

Claudia Gahlinger has written on and about northern Cape Breton Island since 1985. Her first collection, *Woman in the Rock*, which includes the story "Harvest," appeared in 1993. She lives in South Harbour.

Tessie Gillis

Tessie Gillis was born in Montana and brought to Cape Breton in 1950 to restore her husband's family farmstead. Illness eventually gave her time to write, and she produced short stories and two novels. She died in 1972, before any were published. Her complete works are available in two volumes: *Stories from the Woman from Away* and *John R. and Son.*

Ann-Marie MacDonald
Connected to Cape Breton by blood and visits, Ann-Marie MacDonald was born in the former West Germany and grew up on the move. Her first solo-authored play, *Good Night Desdemona (Good Morning Juliet)*, took the Governor-General's Award and the Chalmers Award. Her first novel, *Fall on Your Knees*, has sold over 160,000 copies in Canada alone, and has won the Commonwealth Prize for Best Fiction Novel, the Dartmouth Book Prize for Fiction, and the Canadian Authors Association Award for Fiction.

Beatrice MacNeil
Born in Glace Bay and raised in the village of L'Ardoise, Beatrice MacNeil now lives in East Bay. *The Moonlight Skater*, a book of short stories and a play, received the Dartmouth Book Award. She produces the annual Fiddles and Prose Ceilidh. Her stories have appeared in many publications.

Erin McNamara
Erin McNamara grew up in Glace Bay, eating her mother's chowder and her father's turkey noodle soup. She spent most of her adult life sampling soups and other delicacies in Toronto, while attending university. She returned to Glace Bay for several years to live and work and cook for her daughter. Now attending Queen's University Law School, Erin provides soup for her classmates and forages in the restaurants of Kingston for new material.

Jean McNeil
Co-winner of the Prism International Fiction Competition (1997), and nominated for the 1998 Journey Prize for fiction, Jean McNeil is from Boularderie, Cape Breton. Her fiction and poetry have been published in Canadian and United Kingdom literary magazines. Her novel *Hunting Down Home* was published in the U.K. and Canada in 1996, and in the United States in 1999. She lives in London, England.

Teresa O'Brien
Born in Ireland, Teresa O'Brien makes her home in Cape Breton. "A Trailing Memory" is her first fiction publication.

Sherry D. Ramsey
Devoted primarily to science fiction and fantasy—her work has appeared in Marion Zimmer Bradley's *FANTASY Magazine*—Sherry Ramsey is a former lawyer who decided that the problems of her characters were more interesting than those of her clients. She maintains www.geocities.com/~scriptorium, "a virtual room for writers."

D. C. Troicuk
Born in Glace Bay, D. C. Troicuk has had stories published in *The Antigonish Review*, *Pottersfield Portfolio*, and *Canadian Living*. She lives in Sydney, where

she designs counted cross-stitch kits for her company, Foxberry Cottage Crafts.

Kim Williamson
Born in Cape Breton and raised in a movie theatre, this is Kim Williamson's first published fiction. Her coffee shop, Molasses and Cream Café, promoted local art and a Cape Breton writing group.

Susan Zettell
The author of *Holy Days of Obligation* (1998), Susan Zettell has had stories anthologized in *Quintet* (1998) and in *Spider Women* (1999). While she now makes her home in Ottawa, she continues her attachment to Cape Breton.

ALSO AVAILABLE FROM
Breton Books

STORIES FROM
THE WOMAN FROM AWAY
by TESSIE GILLIS
"It's a very frightening book"—and one of the finest novels Cape Breton ever produced. Presenting a woman's life, and the men and women whose struggles, weaknesses and wit enrich her rural community, it delivers with unparalleled intensity a bold, rare portrait of the Maritimes.
$18.50

JOHN R. AND SON
and Other Stories
by TESSIE GILLIS
No one has ever written about Cape Breton quite like this. A rich, daring short novel, plus 5 stories, this troubling, brutal, compassionate book is a riveting minor classic.
$18.50

THE MOONLIGHT SKATER
9 Cape Breton Stories & The Dream
by BEATRICE MacNEIL
Short stories that blossom—or explode—from a mischievous blend of Scottish and Acadian roots; and her classic rural play.
$11.00

GOD & ME
by SHEILA GREEN
A gentle way of sharing wonder and relationship with a child, and a lovely keepsake for any adult: 18 open, unpretentious poems; 7 drawings by Alison R. Grapes.
$9.00

STERLING SILVER
Rants, Raves and Revelations
by SILVER DONALD CAMERON
Essays from over 25 years of writing, never before in print form—*Sterling Silver* demonstrates a wide range of Silver Donald's interests. From suicide to love and fear, craftsmanship and community—this is Silver Donald Cameron angry, hopeful, incisive and amused.
$21.50

THE GLACE BAY
MINERS' MUSEUM
—THE NOVEL
by SHELDON CURRIE
The movie "Margaret's Museum" has won awards in Spain, Halifax, Vancouver. And the novel behind it all is every bit as haunting and mesmerizing as the movie. Terrific storytelling with a bizarre, shattering ending, it has the guts to carry a love story out in the coal region of Cape Breton to a staggering, realistic conclusion.
$16.25

THE STORY SO FAR...
by SHELDON CURRIE
Finally, a collection of Currie's best stories—disturbing and compassionate. A serious book of high comedy, these 11 stories dare to deal with our terrors and acts of tenderness, from questioning love to wanting love to actually trying to *create* love.
$16.25

• PRICES INCLUDE GST & POSTAGE IN CANADA •

ALSO AVAILABLE FROM
Breton Books

THE LAST GAEL
and Other Stories
by ELLISON ROBERTSON

Shimmering between exuberant humour and almost unremitting darkness, the stories in *The Last Gael* reflect elements of life in Cape Breton, where the traditional and the urban not only coexist but engage one another, often at war in the single person or event. Painter/author Robertson has produced a rich, satisfying book, rooted in the place and the man. These stories have plot, meaning, acute observation—and they are told with quiet, accomplished grace. This is a welcome Maritime voice.

$16.25

ARCHIE NEIL
by MARY ANNE DUCHARME
From the Life & Stories of Archie Neil Chisholm of Margaree Forks, C. B.

Saddled with polio, pride, and a lack of discipline, Archie Neil lived out the contradictory life of a terrific teacher floundering in alcoholism. This extraordinary book melds oral history, biography and anthology into "the triumph of a life."

$18.50

CAPE BRETON WORKS:
More Lives from
Cape Breton's Magazine

From farm life to boxing, from lighthouse tragedies to fishing adventures, from hunting to mining with horses to work in the steel plant—this extraordinary mix of men's and women's lives delivers a solid dose of the tenacity, courage, humour and good storytelling that make a place like Cape Breton work. From Canada's longest-running oral history journal, these Cape Breton voices affirm, entertain, and inspire—and carry our stories to the world. 300 pages of Life Stories • 154 photos

$23.50

THE HIGHLAND HEART
IN NOVA SCOTIA
by NEIL MacNEIL

Celebrating 50 years of a remarkable Cape Breton classic! Told with the pride and joy that only an exiled son can bring to the world of his heart and his childhood, this is wonderful writing about the peace and raw humour of Celtic Cape Breton's Golden Age. Small minds get their comeuppance, pomposity gets leveled, and rip-roaring stories continue to roar. Raised in Washabuckt, Neil MacNeil became an editor of *The New York Times*.

$18.50

FATHER JIMMY
Life & Times of Father Jimmy Tompkins
by JIM LOTZ & MICHAEL WELTON

The abrasive, compassionate, nagging, cranky, inquisitive, generous, and altogether marvelous priest who remains the inspiration and conscience of a worldwide social movement—Father Jimmy was the spiritual father of the co-op movement in Nova Scotia, the regional library system, and co-op housing. In his work among poor fishermen and miners in the '20s and '30s, he encouraged cooperation, self-reliance and adult education to get people to make a difference in their own lives.

$18.50

CASTAWAY ON CAPE BRETON
Two Great Shipwreck Narratives
1. Ensign Prenties' *Narrative* of Shipwreck at Margaree Harbour, 1780 (Edited with an Historical Setting and Notes by G. G. Campbell)
2. Samuel Burrows' *Narrative* of Shipwreck on the Cheticamp Coast, 1823 (With Notes on Acadians Who Cared for the Survivors by Charles D. Roach)

$13.00

Breton Books & Music
Wreck Cove, Cape Breton Island, Nova Scotia B0C 1H0
speclink@atcon.com • http://www.capebretonbooks.com
• SEND FOR OUR FREE CATALOGUE •